Rule and Camryn
A Memphis Love Story

B. Love

Soar young girl. Soar.

www.authorblove.com

For information about bulk purchases, please contact B. Love via email – authorblove@gmail.com

Edited by: Queen B Enterprises

He Ain't Nobody

What was it about love that made its owners try to force it upon those around them?

That's what Camryn was struggling with because of her cousin, Elle. Her sister, Elle. Her best friend, Elle. Her headache, Elle.

Ever since Elle's boyfriend Power proposed a week earlier she had been trying to force love... and his brother Rule down Camryn's throat.

"I can't go through with this," Camryn admitted.

She stood, unzipped her suitcase, and began to quickly remove its contents.

Elle stood, grabbed the bag, and began to repack it.

"Why not?"

"What I look like going to Las Vegas with you and Power and his brother? I'm going to be bored and alone. I don't know this nigga. He already admitted to being crazy. I'm just going to stay here."

Camryn sat back down on her bed and Elle went and sat next to her.

"Look, I'll admit... Rule is a bit... outspoken... but he's a sweetheart. You two are going to get along just fine. You both are loud and crazy. Wild and carefree. You'll have a good time, Cam. I can't get married without you being there. You're not just my cousin. You're my sister. You're my best friend. Please come."

Elle grabbed Camryn's hand and Camryn sighed heavily. When Power proposed to Elle they agreed to get married in Las Vegas. They invited the two people closest to them, Rule and Camryn, to come.

Camryn had been looking forward to meeting Rule on her own terms.

She expected a quick hi and bye to be able to detach herself from her desire for him before it really even began; not a weeklong trip to a completely different state.

And even though she was putting up a fight she wouldn't miss her favorite cousin's wedding for anything in the world. Even if it meant dealing with a man she'd only spoken to on the phone once and had already concluded that he was crazy, possessive, and probably too sexy for his own good.

There was a power, surety of himself and what he had to offer, and control that had captivated Camryn the moment she heard his voice. That conversation was one she would never forget.

"And then he had the nerve to get mad at me because I left," Camryn almost yelled before taking a sip of her smoothie.

Elle met her for smoothies after her workout. She never had a problem being home alone, but now that she'd gotten so used to Power's presence she hated being there without him. Camryn was telling Elle about her latest date and why she refused to see him again.

"Cam, you can't get mad at the man because he didn't talk crazy when someone bumped into you."

"I ain't saying he had to talk crazy to the nigga. I'm just saying I don't feel like I could trust him with me. I don't feel like I could trust him to be my protector. He didn't even look at the nigga crazy. He just acted like he didn't see the shit."

"Maybe he really didn't see it."

"He saw that shit. He didn't have a choice but to see it and feel it because when he bumped into me I bumped into him. Then when I said something to the nigga he gone tell me to chill out. Like he was scared or some shit."

Elle chuckled and shook her head.

"What did you want him to do?"

"Something. He could have just been like, damn nigga, or excuse you, or aye you bumped into my girl. Something. I shouldn't have had to say anything. That's why I deal with street niggas because they have no problem putting a nigga in check, and me too. You know how my attitude is. I can't be with a man that holds back."

"I don't want you with a street nigga anyway."

"I can't be with no other type, Elle. I've tried. I can't find me a man like Power. One that used to be in the streets but is on his good guy swag now. I wouldn't mind that kind."

Elle's mind immediately went to Rule. She didn't know much about him, but being that he was Power's brother she figured they had to be alike in some ways.

"Hmmm… what if I could get you someone like Power?"

"Someone like who?"

"His brother."

Camryn's eyes squinted as she leaned deeper into her seat.

"You mean to tell me this nigga has had a brother all of this time and you failed to mention that and hook a sister up?"

Elle laughed quietly and sat deeper in her seat.

"I'm sorry, Cam. It never crossed my mind."

"Mane, what does he look like? Is he cute?"

"Yes. He's fine. He looks like Power kind of. They're the same brown shade. He's tatted with that bad boy edge that you like. I think you'll like him."

"Get me him."

Elle pulled her phone out and went through her contacts until she found Rule's number. She dialed it and hoped he was still single. Camryn had no problem taking a man that she was interested in. She was hardly ever interested in someone, so when she was… she let nothing or no one stand in the way of that.

"What's up, Elle? Everything good?" Rule spoke.

She understood the worry in his voice. They hadn't spoken since he agreed to not pursue her. The only other time they saw each other was when Elle went to their parents' home for dinner, but they hardly spoke to each other then.

"Yea, everything's good. Umm are you single?"

"Am I single? Yea. You ain't coming for me are you? That would kill Power."

"Hell nah. I'm well satisfied with my baby. I don't want you for me. I want you for my cousin."

"Aw, okay. Is she pretty?"

Elle giggled and looked Camryn over.

"She's my cousin, Rule. What you think?"

"His name is Rule? That's sexy as hell," Camryn mumbled.

"That was her? Her voice sexy as hell. Let me talk to her. Put me on speaker."

Elle put the call on speaker and sat her phone on the table.

"Say hello, Cam," Elle said smiling.

Camryn looked from the phone to Elle.

"Hey," she spoke pulling the phone closer to her.

"You sound good as fuck, Love. How are you?"

Camryn's mouth opened partially as she looked at Elle.

"Say something, crazy," Elle coached.

"I'm good, how are you?"

"I'm better now. I hear you checking for a nigga?"

Camryn frowned and picked the phone up.

"Oh Lord, be nice," Elle said.

"Nigga, I ain't checking for you. I don't even know you. I just wanted to see if you looked as good as your brother."

Rule chuckled and Camryn's frown turned into a smile.

"I've heard that I do a few times. Why don't you let me take you out so you can find out for yourself?"

"I don't know about all of that yet. You could be crazy."

"I am crazy, but you gone love me."

"What makes you think that?"

"I can hear it in your voice. So you gone let me take you out?"

"How about I just meet you at your brother's house one day and we can take it from there? I don't like wasting time and energy."

"I feel the same way, but nothing you ever do with me will be a waste. We can do that, though. What's your name?"

"Camryn."

"Okay, Camryn. I'll let Elle know when I'm going to be over there and you two can swing through. Be looking good too. I'm a man and I'm stimulated by what I see. If you want me come correct."

"I don't want your cocky ass. I can see now we not gone get along."

He laughed again and once again her frown turned into a smile.

"I'll let you know when I'm ready for you, Camryn. In the meantime, cut all your other niggas off so you can prepare yourself for me. I'm possessive as hell."

Camryn looked at the phone as Elle squealed in excitement.

"How are you just going to demand that I cut my niggas off? I'm not yours to possess. You might not even be for me. Why would I cut my niggas off just for you? Besides, you don't know shit about me. You don't even know how I look. You might not even like me."

"Why you like to go against everything I say? I'm gone have to break you of that shit. Just do what I said and let me take care of all that other shit you worried about."

He disconnected the call and Camryn groaned loudly.

"This nigga!" She yelled fanning herself.

"Got you hot, huh? Lord have mercy. What have I done? I think you just met your match, Cam."

"Girl. I don't! His ass mean and crazy! He thinks he's running shit."

"You like it, though."

Camryn's smile covered her face although she tried to hold it in.

"I love it. I can't wait to see his fine ass!"

"So are you going or not? If not, Power and I will just have to get married here or something because I'm not doing it without you," Elle continued, bringing Camryn out of her thoughts.

Camryn released a hard breath and stood.

"Fine, but if this goes horribly wrong it's on your head."

"I will take all the blame," Elle agreed excitedly as she stood. "Now let's go. They've been sitting outside for thirty minutes waiting on you."

"Whatever. I could've met y'all at the airport anyway."

"Don't start with the attitude. I know you only have one because you're scared to finally meet Rule."

"Girl, bye. Ain't nobody scared to meet that nigga. He ain't nobody."

Elle rolled her eyes and grabbed Camryn's smaller bags.

"Whatever. Let's just go before we miss our flight."

Camryn slowly walked behind Elle. As she locked the door behind them she heard a door open and close and she prayed silently that it was Power getting out and not Rule.

"I love you, remember that," Elle whispered with a smile before walking away.

Camryn groaned inwardly and turned around slowly. Her eyes closed immediately at the sight of the man before her.

She figured he would be handsome… but not *this* handsome.

Not so handsome that just the slight glimpse of him made her heart race. Her palms sweat. Her nipples harden. Her bottom set of lips cry.

No... this was beyond what she expected.

Rule took her bag into his hand, brushing his fingers against her knuckles in the process... and in the heat of the summer... his touch had given her chills. She opened her eyes in time enough to watch him lick his lips and take a step back to admire her beauty. Slowly he circled around her and she rolled her eyes.

"Really, nigga? You just gone walk around me like I'm a piece of meat?" She asked walking towards the car.

"I can't look?" Rule asked with a smile.

"Not like that."

"Like what?"

"Like I'm a used car and you're trying to get a full look before you make your decision."

"I can see now your ass gone be dramatic as hell," he observed as he opened the door for her.

She cut her eyes at him before getting inside.

"I am not dramatic. Just don't look at me like that no more."

"Listen, if I see something of value that I'm interested in pursuing I'm going to check it out from all sides. If that bothers you... get over it."

Rule slammed the door and cut Camryn's reply off. This time when she groaned it was loud enough for Power and Elle to hear as she kicked the back of the passenger's seat.

"What's up, Cam?" Power asked with a smile.

"Mane, you better get your brother, or this gone be the longest week in life."

Power chuckled and gripped the steering wheel. "Uh, I don't know if there's much I can do about that crazy ass nigga. Just be patient with him. His mouth is slick and he has no filter, but you're the same way. Just take the time to get to know him, Cam."

Rule opened the door and got in. Camryn looked at him and rolled her eyes, shaking her head in disgust in the process. Rule laughed quietly as he put his seatbelt on.

"You welcome," Rule mumbled as Power drove off and started their journey to the airport.

Camryn turned her head slowly towards him. "For what?"

"I put your shit in the trunk. You welcome."

"I didn't ask you to."

"You want me to get it out so you can do it then?"

"Nigga, Ion care!"

"Nope. I'm driving," Power said.

"Cam... please," Elle added.

Camryn sat back and crossed her arms over her chest.

"Thanks," she muttered.

"I'm sorry... I didn't hear you."

"You heard me."

"No I didn't. You mumbling under your breath and shit. Say it just as loud as you did when you told me that you didn't care."

Camryn smiled but licked her lips in a failed attempt to conceal it as she shook her legs and head.

"Oh wait... was that... was that a smile?" Rule asked, grabbing her chin and turning her face towards him.

"Don't touch me," Camryn ordered as she pushed his hand away from her face. "And yes it was a smile, but it wasn't a happy smile."

"Then what kind of smile was it, Camryn?"

Camryn looked at him and took in his beautiful features once more.

His pecan skin, coffee colored under turned eyes, naturally thick and arched eyebrows, pierced ears, and blunt brown lips all added to his handsomeness, but it was his deep dimples and freckle covered nose and cheeks that she found herself losing herself in.

Those freckles were going to get her in trouble.

Slowly she reached over to him and ran her pointing finger down the curve of his nose, then her pointing and middle fingers against the freckles on his cheek.

Rule licked his lips and showed those dimples that had her nipples hard as small pebbles and she quickly removed her hand. As if she'd just realized what she had done. Sitting on both of her hands she looked straight ahead and mentally cursed herself for displaying her interest in him – even if it was just physically.

Neither of them said anything else for the rest of the ride to the airport.

See-line Woman Dressed in Red

Camryn may have thought her attitude was turning Rule off and pushing him away but it was actually drawing him to her even more. He loved a challenge. He was the rebel that always did the opposite of what others were doing, or what he was told to do. Always going against the grain.

Which is why he took pride in getting under Camryn's skin.

The harder she fought the harder he wanted to pursue.

There wasn't much that she could say or do at this point to turn him off. Camryn was beautiful. Her hair was large, full, curly, and auburn in color. Her skin was the same sandy tan shade as Elle's.

With a slim frame, gray slanted eyes, and the cutest small nose and lips he'd ever seen, Camryn gained Rule's sight in a matter of seconds. Her fiery attitude piqued his interest and caused him to want to see if she could match his vision just as well as she'd caught his sight.

Rule hadn't said anything to her since she helped herself to his freckles. Not because he didn't want to talk to her, but because he wanted her to drown in her desire for him without him saying something to turn her off.

The four checked into the Stratosphere hotel. Power and Elle went to make arrangements for their wedding, leaving Rule and Camryn to entertain themselves. When Rule dropped her bags off in her room he offered to take Camryn to lunch.

He could tell by her facial expression that she agreed out of hunger and not a desire to spend time with him but that didn't faze him at all. After taking a quick shower and getting settled into his room Rule made his way to the restaurant – Top of the World.

Rule grabbed his phone to call back home and check in with his business partner, Yancey, but was caught off guard by the multiple missed calls from his ex, Diana. He broke up with her a month earlier because he questioned her loyalty. There were days when she wouldn't call or text him at all, and then there were days like today when she would consistently reach out to him.

Rule couldn't quite put his finger on any one thing Diana had done wrong, he just couldn't name one thing she'd done right. Because of this he felt as if she was with him for his power, status, and money – not for who he truly was. As he scrolled through his call log for Yancey's number Diana called again.

"Yea?" Rule answered with an attitude.

"I can't believe you actually answered."

"Me either. What you want, D?"

"You."

"What do you want that you can have?"

"So you saying I can't have you?"

"That's exactly what I'm saying."

"But why not? You can't even tell me what I did wrong."

"Just let me go, D. I swear it wasn't that deep. We kicked it for what... a couple of months? Move on."

"I don't want to move on. I miss you, Rule. You got me sprung. You can't just give me the deep dick and spoil me with shopping trips and then just cut me loose. Especially when I didn't even do anything wrong."

"What do I do for a living, Diana?" She was silent. "What part of town do I live in?" Silence. "How old am I? What's my last damn name? Can you tell me one thing about myself?"

Diana breathed heavily into the phone and Rule pulled it from his ear briefly in irritation.

"So we didn't take the time to get to know each other... we can do that now."

"That's just it... I don't want to get to know you, D. It was fun while it lasted, but I just can't see myself growing with you. You have no passion. No drive. No interest in bettering yourself. Hell, you didn't even have any interest in getting to know me. You saw my car and the niggas I was with and hopped on my dick. I ain't with that."

"Then why didn't you just say that? I only had sex with you because I thought you wouldn't give me a chance if I didn't."

"Well... I'm sorry you felt like that."

The red silhouette walking his way caught the corner of his eye. Rule looked to the left and saw Camryn practically floating towards him in a flowing red maxi dress.

His voice was low as he said, "I gotta go," disconnecting the call at the same time.

Rule stood and took all of Camryn in as she took her surroundings in. Her eyes were bright and her smile was wide as she looked past him and out of the window. The restaurant was eight hundred and forty four feet in the air, twisting 360 degrees every eighty minutes. Their table was right next to a window – giving them the perfect view of the Las Vegas skyline.

"This view is gorgeous. How did you get this table?" Camryn asked as he pulled her chair back.

He couldn't help but consider how beautiful his own view was. His view of her. Camryn sat down and looked up at him.

"What, nigga?"

"See-line woman dressed in red. Make a man lose his head," Rule quoted returning to his seat.

Camryn smiled surprisingly. "Nina Simone."

"What you know about that, girl?"

"No. What do *you* know about that? I love me some Nina Simone."

"Me too. She's one of my favorite artists."

"Really? So you're into old school music?"

"My favorite thing to listen to. Really that and Gospel is the only thing I listen to on a consistent basis. I listen to trap music when I'm in the streets or working out, but other than that I gets down with the old school vibes."

"Me too!" Camryn agreed surprisingly. "I can't get with this new age shit. Neosoul I can do, and there are a few new artists I can listen to, but other than that I keep it Gospel and old school."

"Give me your top five old school artists."

Camryn leaned back and looked up at the ceiling in thought. "Umm Nina, Al Green, Otis Redding, Sam Cooke, Ann Peebles. What about you?"

Rule smiled and licked his lips. "You wouldn't believe me if I told you."

"Tell me," Camryn replied leaning forward.

"Nina. Al. Otis. Sam. Marvin Gaye."

"Shut up! Stop lying!"

"I'm serious. Those are my top five. I have just about everything they've created on vinyl."

"Really? I've always wanted to start a vinyl record collection. There's a yellow vinyl record player that I've had my eye own but I haven't purchased it yet."

"Why not?"

She shrugged. "I don't know. I don't really spend too much money on myself. Elle has to force me to buy shit. That's just not my thing."

"So your man spoils you then?"

Camryn's reply was cut off by their waitress coming to take their drink orders. She looked directly at Rule as she asked, "What can I get you guys to drink?"

Rule nodded at Camryn. "Start with the young lady."

She nodded hesitantly before shifting the weight of her body to the right and looking at Camryn.

"What can I get you, hun?"

Camryn chuckled and picked up the menu.

"I don't know. I haven't had time to look. I want a glass of water for sure. And give me a glass of Moscato."

"Can you hold your liquor?" Rule asked.

"Yea."

"Then just order us a bottle of something."

"I don't drink that heavy shit."

"That's cool. Get whatever you want."

"Alright… get us a bottle of Sauternes."

"Yes maim." She turned her attention back to Rule. "I'll go and get that and give you guys some time to look over the menu."

Camryn chuckled as she walked away.

"What's so funny?" Rule asked.

"Nothing."

"Spit it out."

"She wants you."

"No she don't. She's just working on her tip."

"Whatever."

"You jealous?"

"Why would I be jealous, Rule?"

This was the first time he'd heard her say his name. And this was the first time his name sounded so powerful and meaningful.

"What does this wine taste like that you're about to have me drinking?" Rule asked changing the subject.

"Honey."

"You never answered my question."

"What question?"

"Does your man spoil you?"

"I don't have one of those."

"You got rid of them niggas like I said?"

Camryn sat back in her seat and rolled her eyes, failing horribly yet again at holding in her smile.

"There weren't any for me to get rid of really, but I did stop talking to a couple of guys. Not because you told me to either."

"Yea, I hear you."

"Do you always talk like this?"

"Like what?"

"Random. Several topics at once."

"I guess. Never really paid it much attention. Is that a problem?"

"No, not really. I just have to remember not to say anything I don't want you bringing up again."

"I'll still pull it out of you. You don't want to talk about yourself and spoiling yourself?"

Their waitress returned with their wine and Rule couldn't help but notice the look of relief that covered Camryn's face.

"May I suggest something or do you know what you would like to order?" She asked.

"Have you been here before?" Rule asked Camryn.

"Nope. Order for me."

Rule nodded and picked up his menu. "Give her the three course meal. She'll have the Caesar salad, petite filet mignon and mashed potatoes with shrimp scampi, and the chocolate duo. Matter of fact... just give me the exact same thing."

"Yes sir. We'll have it right out." She took both of the menus and walked away.

"How did I do?" Rule asked.

"You did good. That sounds great."

"Cool, so back to my question."

"No I don't like to talk about myself," Camryn answered quickly.

"Why not?"

Camryn shrugged and looked out of the window. "I on know. Just don't."

"Well you gone have to come out of that shit with me."

"Why do you care?" She asked as she turned her eyes back to his.

This time, he shrugged. *Why did he care?*

"I just think you might be of quality substance. I just want to see if I'm right. Niggas don't take the time to get to know you?"

"It's not that. That's just not something I've really been interested in. I kick it with niggas and date... but I ain't for that relationship and commitment and love stuff."

Her answer caught him off guard. Sure he didn't know her... but what woman didn't want love? What woman didn't want to belong to one man and be his alone? He leaned forward into his seat and looked into her eyes as if he could look into her soul. As if he could look into her heart. Camryn fluffed her hair and looked down insecurely. Rule opened the wine and poured her a glass. She drank half of it and released a hard breath.

"So why don't we start there?" Rule asked.

"Why?"

"Why not? Don't fight me on this. You should know by now that I'm very vocal about what I want and I always get it. Just make it easy for the both of us and tell me what I want to know."

"What is this an interview?"

"I guess you could think of it that way. Would that make you feel better? If this seemed less intimate and personal? You want me to stop talking to you like a gentleman and switch up to the hood nigga in me?"

"You're confusing."

"How?"

"I guess I just wasn't expecting this from you."

"What were you expecting?"

"I don't know. For you to be on some fuck shit honestly. I figured you would throw me compliments and mediocre conversation to see what you could get out of me. I guess I expected that because I categorized you."

"Don't misunderstand… I'm very attracted to you physically. And I did want to explore your insides the second I laid eyes on you, but I'm not one of these standard ass niggas. I don't take you blessing me with your presence lightly. I'm not concerned with entering you physically until I have thoroughly fucked you mentally."

Camryn grabbed the wine and refilled her glass. After taking a few long gulps she wiped her mouth and filled it up again.

Rule laughed softly and pulled the wine from her hand.

"I want you sober for this."

"I can't. That was too much."

"You want to stop?"

She bit down on her lip as she looked him over, reminding him of Elle, and shook her head no.

"I think I might like this."

"Good. So start from the beginning. Tell me about you."

Rule poured himself a glass of wine.

"Okay. My name is Camryn Meadows. Elle and I are related on my mother's side. My dad is white. Mom is black. I'm twenty-four. My birthday is June 29th.

I graduated with a double major of Education and African American studies. I teach an African American class at Ridgeway. I want to get my PhD and teach college level courses."

"Does your love for African American studies and culture have something to do with your father being white?"

She nodded sadly.

"Yea. Like… growing up… I was never black enough. I wasn't black enough for blacks and I wasn't white enough for whites. I used to get teased for my light skin and gray eyes. Elle is light skinned too so we had to learn how to fight at an early age because we were so hated.

Hated because of something we had no control over. So I started studying my mother's family and tracing my roots and it just turned into wanting to learn more and more about that part of myself."

"Are both of your parents still living and married?"

"They're both alive but they were never married. My dad couldn't handle the hate that came from being with a black woman so he left and married a white woman."

Camryn chuckled but he could see the sadness in her eyes.

"Did your mother ever marry? How did she handle that shit?"

"She married the first black man to show her some love and affection. He turned out to be married, though. He was separated from his wife for the time being and she didn't even know. By the time she found out she was in love. She played the side chick role before it was cool and acceptable.

Eventually he divorced his wife and married my mama, but he ended up cheating on her too. They divorced when I was fourteen and she hasn't remarried since. My mama... I love that lady, man. She taught me how to be a damn good woman. She taught me how to love myself and respect myself, but she didn't teach me how to choose a man.

How to submit, respect, and love and be loved in a healthy way. I guess that's why I don't really want that now. I don't want to love and trust because I don't want to be hurt and left. Rejected."

"But you gotta know her path isn't yours to take. Just because that happened to her that doesn't mean it's going to happen to you... unless you choose to continue that cycle."

"Yea," she mumbled before taking a sip of her wine.

"You have your own place? Or you stay with your moms?"

"Yea I stay with her. I'm not leaving until I'm married."

"That's cool. What do you like to spend your free time doing?"

"Listening to music. Journaling. Dancing and kicking it with Elle. I need to find a new best friend, though, because she's about to be married and Power gone be taking up all my time."

Her pout made him smile.

"What's your favorite color?"

"Yellow."

"You want me to take up that empty space?"

"Is that a trick question?"

"Not at all."

Their waitress returned with their salads. "Here you are. Your main course will be out soon."

Neither answered right away. Eventually Rule nodded and mumbled a quick thanks, his eyes never leaving Camryn's.

"I would like that. Just don't expect too much from me."

"I'll only expect what you offer to give."

"What if all I have to give is my companionship?"

"That's more than enough for me."

"Cool. Tell me about you." Camryn pushed her plate to the side.

"Rule Owens. Twenty-six. February 20th. Parents are alive and married still. I graduated with a degree in Philosophy. I wanted to go to Law school."

"Really? Why didn't you?"

"Just... never got around to it, but I learned a lot while in school so I don't take it as time wasted. Philosophy teaches me how to understand and analyze situations and go beyond the surface. How to define and interpret situations."

"But you're a drug supplier... right?"

Rule chuckled and hung his head but quickly raised it. "Yea I am. Is that a problem?"

Camryn shrugged and licked her lips.

"I mean… as long as I don't get caught up in it no. I don't plan on marrying you or having no kids with you so what you do is not my concern. It's not my place to try and change you. I do believe in reaching your highest self and your fullest potential, though. It's a part of my nature to nurture and try to pull that out of people, but I would never try to change you.

That's how you get hurt. Falling for the potential of who a person could be or what a situation could be. Then you try to change it or them or expect something they never offered to give. You end up disappointed and hurt and they end up feeling less than."

For a few seconds, Rule just stared at her. Unaware of how to put in words how what she said made him feel. So as not to spoil the moment he remained silent and said nothing at all.

"You mean that shit?" Rule asked just above a whisper.

"I do."

"I deal with frauds on a daily basis. Niggas and females who don't want me but who I am and what I have to offer. They don't want to get to know the real me, and those closest to me who know the real me want to change me. So if you mean that shit I don't give a fuck if you don't want a relationship and love or not. I'm coming after you and we're giving each other both."

"Rule… that's not something I…"

"Did you mean that shit?"

"Yes, but…"

"Then all that other shit don't matter."

"Rule, you can't make me be with you."

He laughed and shook his head before taking a sip of his wine.

"I have my own place and a few businesses. I have a car lot, car wash, and an auto and detail shop."

"Did you hear what I said?"

"You're wearing my favorite color."

"Nigga, you hear me talking to you."

"Yea, I hear you, but you ain't really saying nothing."

"Me telling you that I don't want a relationship doesn't mean anything to you?"

"Pretty much."

Their waitress returned with their main courses. "Is everything okay? Did you guys not like the salads?"

"We haven't started on them yet. Why don't you just bring the dessert in to go boxes and the check as well?"

"Separate checks," Camryn added.

"One check," Rule said as he directed his gaze to Camryn. "Don't start, Camryn."

"Don't start what?"

"That."

"What?"

Instead of answering her Rule turned back to the waitress. "Just bring what I asked for how I asked for it."

"Yes sir."

She walked away. Camryn rolled her eyes and crossed her arms over her chest.

Rule sat back in his seat and shook his head in disappointment. What started out as such a promising lunch left him with no appetite at all for food, but his hunger for her had unfortunately grown even more.

I'm Good

Camryn's eyes watered at the sight of Elle. Elle walked out of the dressing room in what they both knew was the dress. After she and Power secured their wedding space and time at the hotel she met up with Camryn to go dress shopping.

Their last trip was to Celebrations Bridal and Fashion and neither of them thought they would have any luck finding anything – until they set eyes on a Kitty Chen gown that was absolutely stunning. The spaghetti strap lace backless mermaid gown accentuated Elle's curves as it gripped them effortlessly. Elle turned and gave Camryn a glimpse of the ruffled train.

"So…" Elle started as she turned back around. "What do you think?"

"That's the one, boo. That's the one."

Camryn wiped the tears from her cheeks with a smile as Elle did the same.

"You think so? It's not too much is it?"

"Absolutely not. That dress is gorgeous, Elle. It's perfect."

"Okay. Wow. Well… this is the one we're going with then. God… I can't believe this is happening. I'm actually getting married."

"Power is a great man, Elle. I'm so glad you didn't allow your fear to keep you from really giving him a chance."

"You and me both. Here…" Elle turned again. "Help me get out of this." Camryn stood and walked over to Elle.

As she unbuttoned the dress Elle asked, "How did lunch with Rule go?"

Camryn stopped momentarily at the mention of his name then started back on the buttons. Rule opened a box in Camryn's mind and heart that she wasn't prepared to have opened yet. That she didn't plan on opening period. Especially for him.

A man who had her smiling one minute and seething mad the next. A man who had such control over her emotions that she didn't even feel like herself with him. A man who was fully aware of his power as a man. Camryn patted a button softly as if trying to use it to smooth her feelings out.

"It was cool. It started out good. We have the same taste in music. He was surprisingly nice and gentlemanly. But then we got on the subject of him being in the streets and shit went left quickly."

Elle turned around sharply and almost caused Camryn to snatch a button from the dress.

"Have you lost your mind, crazy? I almost ripped that button off."

"What do you mean shit went left?" Elle asked with squinted eyes.

"I mean… he was like… blah blah blah no one accepts me and if you do we're going to be in a relationship and love each other. Like I hadn't just told him that I wanted nothing to do with that."

Elle took a step back. Her eyebrows wrinkled in confusion. Her lips parted as if the words wanted to fall from her lips… but they just… couldn't.

"What?" Camryn asked.

"So you turned him down?"

"I mean… I guess you could say that."

"But you like him?"

"He's cool… when he's not being an ass."

Elle scratched her forehead as her eyebrows relaxed. She turned her back to Camryn and allowed her to return to the buttons.

After a few seconds she asked, "Don't you want this?"

"Want what, Elle?"

"You know what. Love. Marriage. A man who adores you and wants you and you only. Babies."

"When have I ever?"

"When we were kids. We planned our weddings out. Did you forget? I wanted a big fancy wedding with hundreds of people there that I didn't even care to know. But you… you just wanted something small and simple with me, your man, and a Pastor."

"Isn't it funny how people and desires change? Look at you… getting ready to say your vows in front of just me and Rule."

"And look at you… completely closed off from love."

"I'm done," Camryn mumbled sitting back down.

"I'm not telling you to marry Rule. Frankly, I don't know if I could handle that. I'm just saying… if he wants to give you love… why not let him?"

"It's not him loving me that scares me."

"Then what scares you, Cam?"

"Him taking it back."

"You can't be so worried about what may or may not happen in the future that you don't explore this love in your present."

"But it's twice as likely with him. Hell, he could be murdered or go to jail. He could decide he doesn't want to be faithful. He could decide I'm just a challenge and when he gets me he lets me go."

"Or he could fall madly in love with you, leave the game, marry you, and give you babies so our kids can grow up together like we did. We can become sisters for real by marrying brothers."

"This trip isn't about me. This about you and Power. I'm good."

"No you're not... but since you're being stubborn right now and forcing your mother's life on your own I'll let it go for now."

Elle turned and headed back to her dressing room.

Camryn crossed her legs and resisted the urge to step on her train and trip her. Just the thought made her smile and eased the tension building within her.

I Want You

The loud music and never ending chatter of those around her combined with the clinging of machines gave Camryn the effect she desired – no way of hearing her own thoughts. Although they were her own, they were consumed with Rule, and the conversation she had with Elle earlier didn't make it any better. She went to the casino in hopes that the distraction would take her mind off of him.

Camryn sat down at the Wheel of Fortune game and rolled her eyes at the sound of Rule's voice.

"Out of all the shit you could play at the casino you choose Wheel of Fortune?"

She turned around and held her smile in at the sight of his.

"Go away."

"Why?"

"I want to be alone."

"Why?"

"I have to have a reason to want to be alone?"

"Yea." Camryn tried to turn back around but his hand around her forearm stopped her. "You owe me an apology."

"I owe you an apology?"

His hand lowered to hers. She looked down at it and fought to keep from pulling her hand away. Frustrated over the fact that it fit into his perfectly.

"Yes. You owe me an apology."

"Why?"

"Because you ruined my day."

"How did I ruin your day, Rule?"

"We were having a good time until you got in your head and started overthinking the situation."

"I'm not apologizing for that. I told you I didn't want to be in a relationship. You don't listen."

"You gone let me take you to a real casino or you gone continue to waste your time in here? We staying at this hotel for the food and the roller coaster. Oh yea, for the wedding too. Not this dead ass casino. This is Vegas. Stop being so dry."

"I'm perfectly fine where I am. If you want my company for the evening just say that."

"I want you."

Camryn removed her hand from his and stood. His voice. The sincere desire in his tone. His stare. It was becoming too much. She took a step back and clasped her hands together in front of her.

"Well, if we're leaving the hotel I need to go get my purse and phone."

"Fine."

After an awkward moment of silence, she walked past him and made her way back to her room which was conveniently located next to his. They walked side by side and rode the elevator in silence. Camryn quickly went into her room and grabbed her purse and phone. He walked inside quietly. She jumped at the sight of him and stopped walking.

"Pack a light bag," he ordered.

She snickered and shook her head no as she walked towards him. When he didn't move to leave the room her smile faded.

"You… you're not serious."

"Dead ass."

"The hell I need to pack a bag for?"

"We're going to the Venetian."

Camryn opened her arms to the side. "Okay. What is that supposed to mean?"

"Just pack a light bag, Camryn. Why must you always go against what I say?"

"I'm not fucking you."

"I'm not asking you to. I told you what I wanted to do to you. Just pack the bag and come on."

"And I'm not sleeping in the same bed as you."

Rule smiled and shook his head. "That's what you saying now."

"I'll be saying it then too."

"We'll see when we get there."

"How long are we staying?"

"Depends on you."

Throwing all caution to the wind, Camryn grabbed her smaller bag from the closet and packed it. Repeating over and over in her head – *what happens in Vegas stays in Vegas.*

Can I Touch it?

Rule and Camryn checked into their Piazza Suite at the Venetian hotel and casino and neither wanted to leave. The suite had a fully furnished living room area with an open bar.

Their bedroom was beautifully decorated with a stunning view of the city, a king sized bed topped with Egyptian cotton sheets, a bedroom bench that Camryn splattered her body over, and a forty-inch flat screen TV.

The bathroom was equipped with a separate jetted tub and glass enclosed shower and his and hers sinks.

After they convinced themselves to go down to the casino they ended up staying for hours playing craps, blackjack, roulette, and various slots. They ended their night with drinks from the Bellini Bar and headed back to their room for a late dinner.

While Camryn waited for their food to arrive she showered and left Rule alone with his thoughts. Thoughts about her. Rule grabbed his room key and stepped outside to call Power.

"Nigga, where you been? I called your ass three hours ago," Power informed Rule without even saying hello.

"My fault. I left my phone in the room. I was at the casino with Cam."

"What casino?"

"The Venetian."

"You went without me?"

"Yea, nigga. I'm tryna see what's up with her."

"Y'all coming back to the hotel or staying there?"

"Staying here. I reserved the suite just up until the wedding. If we can get along for the next couple of days we gone stay here. Otherwise I'm bringing her ass back."

Power laughed and Rule smiled.

"So y'all keeping y'all rooms here?"

"Yea for now. I don't trust her moody ass. One minute she be smiling in a nigga face like she really enjoying my company then she switch up on me."

The clacking of plates gained Rule's attention. He looked down the hall and saw what he hoped was their room service being delivered.

"Just be careful with her. Elle told me that she's stubborn and strong as hell mentally but that's only because she's easily broken. So don't play with her. Be honest and upfront about what you want with her."

"Aren't I always?"

"Whatever, nigga. Y'all meeting us tomorrow?"

"Yea that's cool. Just hit me up when y'all get up."

"Aight cool."

Rule disconnected the call and looked back at the man pushing the cart of food.

"Is that for room 229?" Rule asked.

"Yes sir. If you could just open the door for me, I'll set everything up in your dining area."

"Cool, 'preciate you."

Rule opened the door and held his hand up to keep the attendant from following him.

"One second," he mumbled closing the door behind him.

Camryn was seated on the bench in nothing but a towel. Her hair was wet and dripping as she massaged her vanilla almond body butter into her feet. Rule leaned against the door and licked his lips, losing himself in the sight before him.

"Go in the bathroom while this dude sets the food up. I don't want him looking at you. And don't put lotion on any other part of your body. I'll handle that."

"I'm not letting you touch my body," Camryn muttered as she stood and headed for the bathroom.

Rule waited until she closed the door before opening the front door and letting the attendant in.

"Sorry about that," Rule apologized as he rolled the cart in.

"No worries. Are you enjoying your stay so far?"

"Yea, it's cool. What would you suggest for breakfast in the morning?"

"My favorite dishes are the steak and eggs and the chicken and waffles, but our griddle items are delicious as well. You can get Belgian waffles, pancakes, or French toast with your choice of fruit topping."

"Cool."

Rule looked back at the bathroom and allowed his mind to roam as the attendant placed their pizza and pasta on the table. Rule stepped closer to him and read his nametag.

"Eric, you wouldn't happen to be working in the morning would you?"

"No sir, but I'm always available to assist. How can I help you?"

"With my breakfast in the morning... I need a dozen long stemmed red roses delivered along with it." Rule pulled his wallet from his pocket and handed Eric a hundred dollar bill. "Can you handle that for me?"

"Yes sir. I'll pick them up in the morning and deliver them personally."

"Perfect. Thanks."

"My pleasure. Thank you." Eric sat their drinks on the table and grabbed his cart. "Enjoy your night, sir."

"You as well."

The second the door closed behind him Camryn asked, "Can I come out now?"

Instead of answering her Rule went to the bathroom and opened the door. She stood and smiled at him. Rule grabbed the front of her towel and pulled her body closer to his.

Camryn stared into his eyes for a split second before covering his hand with hers and grabbing it.

"What are you doing?" Camryn asked softly.

"I don't know." He sniffed the air twice and Camryn lowered her eyes. "Didn't I say don't put no more of that lotion on?"

"I thought that was a joke."

"Your ass ain't think that was no joke. You just hardheaded. Why do you like to give me such a hard time?"

"I told you I didn't want you touching my body."

"Why not?" His hand cupped her cheek. "I'll be so fucking good to it, Cam, I swear."

He'd never heard his voice so low. So husky. So desperate.

Rule took a step back and put some space between them. This wasn't a part of his plan. He didn't want to make love to her – yet. He wanted to show her that she could let her walls down with him by forcing her to give him her undivided time and attention.

"I'm sorry. I'll be less…"

"Against me," Rule offered.

"Yea. Against you. But I still don't want a relationship."

Rule released her and walked away.

She watched him sit down and open his drink before scratching her head and walking over to the sink. After putting her hair up in a ball Camryn walked over to the bed and picked up the shirt Rule had on earlier.

Camryn brought it to her nose, closed her eyes, inhaled his scent, then headed back to the bathroom. When she came back wearing nothing but his shirt Rule sat back in his seat and smirked.

"Why you got my shirt on?"

"Because I like the way you smell and when I sleep tonight it'll make me feel like you're holding me."

Her honesty took him by surprise. Even though he knew that was the reason why, Rule was sure she'd give him a half ass explanation if she gave one at all.

"Or I could just hold you and you can experience the real thing."

Camryn shook her head no as she met him at the table.

"That's too much. I told you I wasn't sleeping with you anyway. Why didn't you get a room with two beds?"

"They ain't have none."

"Liar." Rule smiled and motioned for her to sit down. "Bless the food."

"Gracious and eternal God thank you for this food that we're about to receive. Bless the hands that prepared it and the hands that are receiving it. Please remove anything that might cause our bodies any harm. In Jesus name we pray, amen."

Camryn opened her eyes and looked at him skeptically as she grabbed a piece of pizza and put it on his plate.

"What, mane?" Rule questioned.

"Nothing I just… that was an *actual* prayer."

Rule chuckled and shook his head. "What did you expect? Some God is great God is good foolishness?"

"Yes! I don't know. You just keep surprising me."

"I ain't the best nigga in the world but I do understand the importance of living a right life and having a relationship with God. I fall short and shit but I pray and read my bible throughout the day. I ain't where I want to be, but He ain't finished working on me."

"So your scriptural tattoos aren't just for show then, huh?" Camryn asked before taking a bite of pizza.

"Nah." Rule looked at his tattooed arms and ran his hand down his chest absently. "My brand ain't either."

"Your brand?"

"Yea, I got a cross branded on my chest."

"Let me see."

Rule pulled his shirt over his head and showed his muscular chest, along with the scar from his branding right in the center of it.

"Can I touch it?" Rule nodded. Camryn stood and walked over to him. Slowly she ran the tips of her fingers over the cross. "Why?"

Rule shrugged as he lifted her feet into the air and sat her on his lap.

"It humbles me. Reminds me of the pain he sustained for me. With the life I live I could kill or be killed or get locked up at any minute. It reminds me to be mindful and aware. Thankful for every breath. Every day of freedom."

"Why choose to live like that, though? Why won't you just leave the streets?" Camryn moved her fingers from the cross to the freckles on his face.

"Honestly... it's addictive. I love the rush of it. Nothing has ever made me feel as alive and fulfilled and powerful as the streets do... until I met you. But you throw a nigga such shade the little bit of a rush you give me leaves as soon as you piss me off."

Camryn smiled and wrapped her arms around his neck.

"Normally I'd say some slick shit back, but I said I was going to stop giving you such a hard time so I'm just going to keep that comment to myself."

"Good. You tryna be that for a nigga or what?"

"Rule... I told you I didn't wan –"

Rule took her top lip into his mouth. His hands covered her neck and he arched it slightly. Giving himself deeper access to the inside of her mouth. Gently he spread her lips with his tongue to see if she would allow him entrance.

When she didn't resist Rule slid his tongue into her mouth and connected hers with his.

Her hands slid down his chest as their tongues swayed around each other.

Rule's hands went from her neck to her breasts to her ass – squeezing firmly and pulling her deeper into his pelvis.

Camryn moaned and pulled away from him abruptly.

Her hands covered his and she removed them from her body. She stood and placed her hand on the table for support as she dragged her feet back to her seat.

"I'm sorry. I didn't mean to get that deep," Rule mumbled before running his hands down his face.

"You don't have to apologize. I've wanted to kiss you since I first looked at your lips."

"Why didn't you?"

"Because I didn't like you. Besides, I don't usually move this fast."

"So you saying you like me now?"

"I ain't saying all that."

"Camryn."

"Okay, okay. I like you."

"What does time have to do with it? If you want me... have me. And I like you too."

He watched the smile slowly spread across her face and it caused him to smile.

"I'm still not sleeping with you, though."

"Mane, please. You better throw that long ass pillow between us if need be."

"But, Rule, I told you I didn't want to sleep with you."

"And I told your hard of hearing ass they didn't have no more rooms."

Your Pages Are Beautiful

What was supposed to be a night of not sleeping together turned into half of Camryn's body being tossed over Rule's.

Initially, Camryn stood firm and kept the pillow between them, but after having to constantly pull Rule's hand from her back and placing it back on his side of the bed she gave in, removed it, and scooted closer to him. Rule willingly accepted her closeness and pulled her even closer.

Now that Rule was trying to remove himself from her grip to answer the door he was having a hard time doing so. Every time he inched closer to the edge of the bed Camryn moved right along with him.

"Baby, let me go so I can get the door," Rule said finally.

Camryn whined and released him, turning over to her side in the process.

Rule opened the door and let Eric in. Eric rolled the cart in as quietly as he could after handing Rule the roses. He tried to hand Rule his change, but Rule waved him off.

"Thanks, sir," Eric whispered.

Rule nodded and waited until Eric left before washing his face and brushing his teeth. Afterwards Rule grabbed Camryn's plate along with the roses and sat them both on the bedside table. He sat next to her on the bed and rubbed her back softly.

Camryn shifted slightly but made no effort to open her eyes or sit up. Rule smiled and leaned down, kissing her cheek a few times until she pushed his face away.

"Are you always this grumpy when you wake up?"

Rule slid his hand under the shirt she was wearing and rubbed her back.

"I ain't woke yet."

"So you still sleep?"

"Yea."

"How you talking then?"

She opened her eyes and quickly closed them again with a smile.

"It's too early, Rule. You too live."

"How am I live? Get your lazy ass up and eat with me."

Camryn slurred inaudible words under her breath as she rolled to the opposite side of the bed and made her way to the bathroom. After brushing her teeth and washing her face she walked to the table dreamily.

"Over here, crazy," Rule instructed through his chuckle.

Camryn opened her eyes fully and looked towards his face. The sight of him shirtless holding a bouquet of roses made her close her eyes and pull her hands over her face. Shaking her head in disbelief Camryn refused to cry.

No man had ever given her flowers before.

She was sure one may have decided to try, but once she told them that she didn't want any type of commitment they put in little to no effort and energy. Rule, no matter how many times she said she wanted nothing to do with love and a relationship refused to allow her to deny him of what and who he obviously wanted.

And as much as Camryn hated to admit it... in just the course of a day and a half he was already beginning to change her mind.

Rule gave her a few seconds to compose herself, then placed the flowers on the bed and walked over to her. Kneeling, he pulled her hands down and cupped them between his.

"What's wrong, Cam?"

"Nothing," Camryn mumbled as she opened her eyes. "Nothing's wrong. It's right and that scares me."

"I understand, but are you going to allow that fear to keep you from experiencing what I'm trying to offer you? I'm not your father. I'm not your step-father. You're not your mother.

This is about Rule and Camryn. We ain't gotta get deep. I'm just trying to love on you and get the same in return."

"Promise me that if you begin to lose interest in me that you won't cheat. You won't switch up on me. You won't just randomly leave me without giving me closure. If there's someone else that you want don't fuck off behind my back.

Tell me straight up. Promise me that you'll be a man about it and tell me straight up that this is no longer what you want."

"None of that is going to happen."

"You don't know that."

"Yes I do."

"How do you know?"

"I don't want to tell you."

Camryn tried to remove her hands from his unsuccessfully.

"What you mean you don't want to tell me?"

"You gone same some crazy shit back or you're not going to take me seriously. Just because you don't want to accept your feelings doesn't mean I'm going to let you fuck over mine."

"I'm not going to, Rule. Tell me."

"When I held you last night I felt like the part of me that I've been missing and searching for had made its way back to me. I felt whole."

She lowered her head, but he grabbed her chin and forced her to look at him as he continued.

"So letting go of you would be like letting go of myself, and if it's taken me this long to find that piece of me I ain't letting it go just for the hell of it. Trust me when I say you have no reason to fear me."

Camryn ran her fingers down his freckled cheek before leaning forward and kissing his forehead.

"Okay, I'll try, but I'm going to need some time."

"That's all I'm asking for. Why do you think I kidnapped you?"

She smiled as he stood and lifted her to her feet.

"Thank you for the flowers, Rule. For all of this. You just… keep surprising me. I can't lie I definitely judged you by your cover and your profession but your pages… your pages are so beautiful. So refreshing and unexpected."

"I need you to not worry about this book ending either. Just enjoy every page and trust that even if it does end it will be with a happily ever after."

Camryn picked up the flowers and inhaled their scent. Instead of answering him with her words she wrapped her arms around his waist and answered him with her lips.

Promises

After breakfast, Camryn and Rule returned to the Stratosphere. The minute Camryn tossed her bag onto her bed and sat down there was a knock on her door. With a small smile she went to let Elle in. Camryn opened the door and Elle looked her over before walking into her room. Elle sat on the bed and watched Camryn walk towards her.

"Well… y'all didn't have sex. So what happened?" Elle questioned.

"How you know we didn't have sex?" Camryn asked leaning against the dresser.

"You don't have that sex walk. And if Rule is anything like Power… you'd have it. So what happened? Give me all the details before we meet them," Elle ordered patting the bed for Camryn to sit next to her.

Camryn sat down and let out a hard breath. "Girl, Rule is… nothing like what I expected."

"Is that good or bad?"

"I don't know yet."

"What do you mean you don't know yet?"

"I mean... I thought he was going to be this cocky douche that I couldn't stand. I thought we'd fuck around because we were attracted to each other physically but eventually it would fizzle because there was no substance there... but he's not as big of a jerk as I thought he would be."

She cupped her hands together and twirled her thumbs around each other.

"He's sweet and attentive. He's deep and well rounded. I don't know. He's just... confusing as hell."

"But that's... that's good. I'm not understanding the problem here."

"Elle, you know I don't want to fall in love. I don't want marriage. I don't want kids. He has me rethinking that."

"Again... I'm totally lost on what the problem is."

Camryn rolled her eyes and turned slightly to face Elle. Elle did the same.

"What if he cheats? What if he leaves? What if he goes to jail? What if he dies?"

"Didn't we already have this conversation?"

She turned away and pouted. Elle grabbed her hand and pulled it into her lap.

"Listen... I'm not downplaying your fear... but weren't you the one telling me not to let what Rico did keep me from being loved by Power? You can't let what your father and step-father did keep you from being loved by Rule. Hell... forget love.

Just date the nigga and give that a chance first. Don't overthink this. Don't make it more than what it is… but don't deny what it is either. Have fun. You're in Vegas with a sexy ass nigga! At least rent his ass out until we get back to Memphis."

"I am not having sex with that nigga, Elle. I already know he gone have my ass sprung."

"Fine. But damn just loosen up a bit. Where's my old Cam? The fearless outspoken wild and carefree woman? Where she at?"

"I don't know, but I'll find her."

"Good. Can you find her on the way down the elevator? I want us to have some fun today."

Camryn stood and sighed.

"I'll see what I can do. You go on down to the lobby. I'll meet y'all down there."

"Cool."

Camryn waited until Elle was gone before calling her mother. She grabbed her purse and slowly walked out of the room.

"Hey, baby. You having fun?" Brenda spoke.

"Yes maim."

"You don't sound like you're having fun. What's wrong?"

Her eyes watered as she smiled at how well her mother knew her.

"Nothing's wrong. It's just… there's this guy…"

"Stop right there. He's not your father, Camryn."

"I know, Ma. But I can't just ignore what he did to you."

"To me, baby. What he did *to me*. Your father is a good man, he's just… a weak man. There's nothing wrong with that. He just… couldn't handle being with a strong black woman. He couldn't handle dealing with a strong black woman's family."

"Okay… then what about Anthony? He's black. He still messed you over."

"Me. He messed *me* over. Not you."

"But I'm just like you. So who's to say these niggas won't do it to me?"

"You're not even giving them a chance to. Baby, you're twenty-four years old and you haven't had a boyfriend since you were in high school. Will I ever get some grandbabies?"

"Ma, now is not the time."

"Who is this man? Is it Power's brother that Elle was telling me about? Reign?"

"Rule, Ma."

"Oh. Well I was close. I want you to enjoy yourself, baby. Have fun. Give him a chance. Forget what you think could go wrong and just focus on what's going right. Are you having a good time with him? Is he respectable?"

"Yes maim."

"Then that's what I want you to focus on. How many days left do you guys have there?"

"Including today… four."

"I want you to promise me something."

"What?"

"Promise me first."

"No, Ma. That's not how it works. You have to tell me what it is first."

"Promise me."

"Fine. I promise."

"For the next four days... I want you to live as if I'm not your mother. Edward isn't your father. And Anthony never existed."

"Ma..."

"I'm giving you permission to live as if you don't have any home training. I want you to go crazy. I want you to have the best time of your life. I want you to experience all this man has to offer."

"But what if he hurts me?"

"It will make your stronger. It will show you that you can survive. And knowing that you're a survivor will give you courage. It will make you brave. Not just in love... but in all things. It will show you that it is better to experience love for but a minute than to never experience it at all.

You know... I don't regret anything that I experienced with Anthony and Edward because for two brief moments in life I was able to love unconditionally. I was able to cater to a man who appreciated and cherished me.

It might not have ended the way I wanted it to... but while it was good it was great. And that was more than enough for me.

I'm not single because I'm afraid, baby. I'm single because I've had my fill. I'm satisfied. I've experienced love from men. I've been with men that you have no idea about. Now… I'm just focused on loving God. I want you to step outside of your box and try something new, baby. Can you do that for Mommy?"

"Okay, Ma. I'll give it a shot… just until we get home. I don't want to get attached. As long as I don't get attached I won't get hurt. You can't lose what you've never had."

Brenda chuckled.

"What's funny?"

"Love has no timeframe, baby. It can't be turned on and turned off. Elle told me all about this man, and if he's as good of a match for you as she thinks he is… you won't be able to just… cut him off."

"Ma… what you tryna do? Set me up?"

"I'm trying to get you to *open* up. If you won't give this a fair chance on your own I'm going to make you. Now… a promise is a promise. So, for the next four days I want you to live as if you're not afraid."

"Fine, Ma. I can't believe you're forcing me to wild out."

"Well… sometimes you gotta do what you gotta do. It's not necessarily about wilding out, but what's going to happen during the process. Chains of fear of lost and rejection and being hurt will be broken. Those roots of detachment and lack will be loosed.

I want you to keep an open mind. If this doesn't lead to lasting love, I declare that it will prepare you for the man and relationship that will. I love you, baby. Just trust what I say and not what I've gone through. That was for my testimony... not yours. Enjoy yourself. I'll see you when you get home."

"I love you too."

Camryn disconnected the call and laughed quietly. If anyone could talk her into opening her heart... it would be the woman whose life caused her to close it.

"Fine, Ma. I'll give this shit a try for four days... but I'm going to prove to you and Elle... I can live without a man's love," she muttered to herself as she stepped on the elevator.

The Throne

It was no secret... Rule loved the life he was living. He was the King of Memphis. There was just one problem – he didn't have a Queen or an Heir to his throne. His legal throne that is. If there was one thing that he could change about his life that would be it.

Rule had had his fair share of women in his short life because of his passion for love and acceptance... but he had yet to find a woman who could truly hold his interest... until Camryn. Even with their first phone conversation he knew there was something different about her. There was something in the tone of her voice as she spoke to him that let him know that she was someone he needed to keep around.

Who he was didn't make her approach him or retreat from him. What he had didn't make her cling to him. She didn't care about his status. She respected herself and her body, and she presented a challenge that he willingly accepted.

No... he wouldn't say that he was in love just yet... but he would most definitely say that he was committed to exploring every level of her that he possibly could.

He stepped away from their patio table at Lavo to check in with Yancey but disconnected the call when Camryn made her way to their table. He walked up just in time to hear her ask...

"Where's my freckle face?"

Rule blushed as he wrapped his arm around her stomach and whispered, "You miss me already?"

Camryn turned around to face him and he wrapped his free arm around her as she wrapped hers around his neck. She nodded and bit down on her bottom lip.

"My mama told me to wild out and enjoy myself while I'm here."

"Thank God for your mama. What you wanna do tonight when we split from them?"

"Whatever you wanna do I'm down."

"Aight. We'll come up with a plan after lunch then."

"Are we going back to the Venetian?"

"Sure. You wanna just check out and stay there?"

"Yea, that's cool."

Rule looked at her skeptically for a few seconds before nodding and pulling her seat back. Camryn sat down as Elle cheesed widely.

"You called Aunty? What she say?" Elle whispered.

"Girl... too much. I'll tell you about it later."

"Cool," Elle agreed as their waiter approached their table.

Rule ordered chicken and waffles for himself and Nutella and banana crepes for Camryn. The two couples enjoyed their brunch together and parted ways for what they both knew would be an eventful and entertaining day.

Did I lose you?

Rule and Camryn went to the Mob Museum in downtown Las Vegas. They spent hours in the simulated gun range, visiting different exhibits and reading about criminals on the wall of infamy such as – Al Capone, Virginia Hill, Bumpy Johnson, and Stephanie St. Clair.

After that, they went to the Adventuredome amusement park. Hours later, after they'd ridden every roller coaster, they returned to the suite. Camryn showered and stretched across the bed. While she waited for Rule to shower and return to her she dozed off, but was awaken by the vibration of his phone.

Her eyes went from the phone to the bathroom door until it stopped vibrating. She laid back down just as the phone began to vibrate again. Allowing her curiosity to rule, Camryn grabbed his phone from the bedside table to see who was calling.

"Diana…" She mumbled as the name and picture covered his screen.

Instead of answering as she desired to, Camryn sat the phone back down and rolled to the opposite side of the bed. Its pulse signaled a text message. She licked her lips and looked from the phone to the bathroom door again.

Slowly she rolled back over to the table and picked the phone up. Rule cutting the water off in the shower stopped her from looking at the text message. Camryn hurriedly put the phone back on the table and turned her back to the bathroom door.

Rule's presence filled her nostrils with his Bleu de Chanel. She inhaled it deeply and sighed heavily as she closed her eyes.

"You in for the night, or you wanna get some drinks or something at the casino?" Rule asked sitting on the bed.

Camryn turned slightly and took in his wet bare back before turning back around. Suddenly disgusted and disappointed with no valid explanation in her head as to why. In her head she knew they weren't a couple and they'd just begun to hang out... but that didn't stop her heart from feeling bruised and betrayed.

"I'm done," she mumbled – in more ways than one.

"What's wrong?"

"Nothing."

"Don't lie to me. I hear it in your voice."

Rule grabbed her by the back of her neck and pulled her to the middle of the bed.

"Nigga, don't be handling me like I'm a rag doll," Camryn ordered.

"The fuck is your problem, Camryn?"

"Nothing."

"So that's what we on now?"

She crossed her arms over her chest and silently refused to answer.

"Camryn, if you don't tell me what the hell has put you in this dry ass mood I'm gone drag your little ass out this bed and hang you over the railing on the patio."

She chuckled and shook her head in disbelief.

Rule stood and walked over to his bag. The towel that he had wrapped around his waist dropped and exposed his firm round ass.

Camryn didn't want to look… but how could she not? Her legs opened and closed without her permission as she watched him dig around for a pair of boxers.

When he found them he put them on and turned to walk back to the bed. Camryn quickly turned her face to avoid his eyes.

Rule looked at her from the end of the bed for a few seconds before grabbing her by her right ankle and pulling her to him.

"Rule! Let me go!" She yelled as he grabbed her and tossed her over his shoulder effortlessly.

He didn't let her go. He carried her to the patio as if her fighting to be free felt like nothing against the weight of his body. Rule slid the patio door open and Camryn squealed.

"Okay, okay! I'll tell you. Just… put me down."

Rule stood there briefly, as if he didn't believe her, then he turned around and placed her back in the middle of the bed.

"Talk," he demanded, crossing his arms over his chest and looking down at her.

Instead of speaking, Camryn grabbed his phone and tossed it to him. Rule grabbed the phone and Camryn watched as his facial expression changed.

"Really, Camryn? You tripping because of her?"

"Who is she and why is she blowing your phone up?"

He smiled and licked his lips.

"Come here."

She shook her head no as tears filled her eyes. Not out of sadness but fear. Fear of what she was feeling.

"Come here, baby."

Camryn crawled towards Rule slowly. When she made her way to the edge of the bed she sat on her knees so that they were face to face. Rule cupped her face and ran his thumb over her cheek as he stared into her eyes.

"Have I not been spending every moment with you?" He asked softly.

She covered his wrist with her hand and closed her eyes.

"Yes," Camryn whispered.

"The fuck would I be wasting my time for if I wanted someone else?"

Her eyes opened and met his.

"Who is she?"

"My ex. Really she's not even an ex. We fucked and that's it. I blew a few stacks on her but we were never committed to each other. She can't get the fact that I've moved on through her head, but I don't want her, Camryn. I want you."

Rule removed his hand from her face and dialed Diana's number.

"What are you doing?"

Rule put the call on speakerphone. Diana answered and Camryn rolled her eyes.

"Rule... did you like my picture?"

"D, don't be sending me no pictures of you. Don't send me shit period. Don't text me. Don't call me. I'm done. If I have to tell you that again... fuck it, I'm not gone tell you that again. I'm just gone get my number changed."

"But why? We had something good between us, Rule."

"No... *you* had something good. I wasn't getting shit out of that. Just let me go, Diana. I'm with my lady right now and if I dan lost her because of your clingy ass I'm fucking you up when I get to Memphis."

"Your lady?"

"Did I lose you?" Rule asked Camryn as he ignored Diana's question.

"You never had me to lose me."

Rule disconnected the call.

"So you shutting down on me again? Fine. Did I lose my chance to have you?"

"I'm not the one, Rule. You know how scared I am to be played. If you fuck off of me..."

"I'm not going to do that, Camryn. I have absolutely no desire to play with you or fuck off on you. I've been nothing but straightforward and honest with you. That shit ain't gone change.

If I was fucking with her or anybody else I'd tell you but I'm not. I'm trying to bear with you and help you work through this shit but I'm not gone suffer because of your daddy issues."

She chuckled and pushed him to the side so she could get out of the bed.

"Daddy issues?" She repeated as she snatched her clothes from the chair and threw them into her bag.

"I'm sorry. I didn't mean that. I mean... I meant it... but I didn't mean it in a bad way. You *do* have daddy issues. You think a nigga gone do you wrong and reject you because of what he did but that ain't me."

Camryn went into the bathroom and grabbed her toiletries. Rule sat on the bed and watched her. When she was done packing she went back into the bathroom to put her clothes back on.

"So that's it? You're done trying? You just gone leave?"

Rule stood and walked over to her. Camryn took a step back and hung her head to avoid his eyes. He lifted her head by her chin, but she closed her eyes to avoid his.

"Look at me, baby."

"No," she whined as she felt her emotions begin to completely unstitch.

"Why?" His voice was so low. So distressed. Weak yet heavy. "Cause shit got real? Cause you can't avoid how you feel? Cause a bitch called me and got you in your feelings? I don't want her, Camryn. I want you. How many times do I have to fucking say that?"

"But for how long? Until we get back to Memphis? Until you get bored with me too? You probably gone do me the same way you did her."

"Camryn, if that was the case your ass would still be at the Strat. I would've fucked you and left your ass alone the first day."

She shook her head in disbelief and took a step back.

"I gotta go."

"Go where?"

"Back to the Stratosphere."

"You checked out remember?"

"I'll get another room. If I have to sleep on Power and Elle's couch until the morning I will."

"Nah." Rule took a step back. "You stay here, Beautiful. I'll go."

Rule turned away from her and began to pack his bag. With each piece of clothing he packed it felt as if her heart was pulling back layers.

"This is your room, Rule. I don't mind leaving."

He remained silent as he went into the bathroom and grabbed the rest of his belongings.

"Rule… I can leave," she offered as she grabbed her bag and took small steps to the door.

"I said you ain't leaving. It's midnight. Just… stay here. I'll go."

"Where are you going to go?"

"Why do you care?" The coldness in his voice sent chills down her spine.

"Fine," she muttered as she put her bag down and walked back over to the bed.

Rule pulled his key to the suite from his pocket and placed it on the dresser before stealing one last glance at her and leaving.

Camryn laid down and stared at the ceiling for a few seconds before hopping out of bed, slipping on her flip flops, grabbing the key to the suite, and rushing out of the room – and into Rule's chest.

"Where the hell you going with just a t-shirt on?" Rule asked, pulling at her shirt gently.

She opened her mouth to respond... but found nothing would come out.

"Camryn..."

"I was coming for you."

Rule exhaled a hard breath and took a step back.

"I don't like leaving shit unsettled and going to sleep mad cause that'll just fuck up my day tomorrow. So... I'm sorry."

"You have nothing to apologize for."

"I know."

Camryn smiled and bit down on her lip.

"I'm sorry, Rule. I... freaked out. I'm sorry."

"It's cool. Gone back in the suite before a nigga come out here looking at you and shit."

"You're not coming back?"

"Nah. I think it's best if we just... put some space between us."

"Oh." Camryn took a step back. "Okay. Bye."

She turned, but he grabbed her arm and pulled her into him. After running his fingers down her face he mumbled, "It's goodnight. Not goodbye."

"Right." Her smile was small and forced as she pulled herself from his grasp. "Goodnight."

She dragged her feet towards the room. Each step away from him feeling like daggers along her exposed heart. This… was slowly becoming what she was most afraid of, and she had no one to blame but herself and her fear.

Gentleman with a Savage Attitude

The start of Camryn's day was draining. Instead of being happy as she prepared for the joyous occasion of her cousin's wedding she found herself being consumed by regret. Regret of how she allowed her fear to rob her of Rule. Her heart ached to have him near... but her mind forced her to keep pushing him away.

Elle's light knocking on the door felt like pounding on her heart. She stood and forced a smile but knew Elle would see straight through it.

"Thanks for letting me get ready in here, boo," Elle spoke as she walked into Rule and Camryn's suite.

"It's cool. Are you ready? You're two hours away from becoming Elle Owens."

Elle sat her bags on the bed and sat down.

"Yea... but right now... I want to talk about why Rule was knocking on our door a little after midnight. What happened?"

Camryn rolled her eyes and went to the patio door to look outside. If the reason was as simple as Elle's question made it out to be... he wouldn't have left.

"It's your wedding day and you're worried about my petty drama?"

"Hell yea. You're my girl. Besides... we're heading for the airport right after the wedding. So spill it."

She turned around and leaned against the glass door. How do you put in words the battle of heart vs. mind?

"I lost it. I was paranoid and I almost spazzed."

"Why, though?"

"Some bitch name Diana was blowing his phone up. Calling, texting, then she sent him a picture. That shit bothered me."

Elle chuckled and shook her head.

"So you mad because of something someone else did? Not even what he did?"

With a pout Camryn mumbled, "I was."

"How did he handle the shit? What he say?"

"I mean... he was... he handled it well I guess. He got a little irritated... but he left before it turned into anything. Then he came back and apologized." She chuckled and shook her head as she cupped her hands together. "Like he was the one who did wrong. But it wasn't really about that. It was just the idea of him fucking off with somebody else that scared me."

"Camryn..."

"I know we're not in a committed relationship. And I know I shouldn't feel possessive of him. And I know I shouldn't have been mad at him because a female was blowing his phone up. But I was just paranoid. Scared as fuck that he was cheating and we aren't even in a relationship."

She smiled bitterly and sat next to Elle.

"He probably doesn't even want to talk to me anymore. He probably thinks I'm crazy."

"Yea… he thinks you're crazy."

"What did he say?"

Elle stood and began to unpack her bags.

"He was just like, 'Yo… your cousin is crazy as hell, Elle. I like her crazy ass though.' I asked him what happened and he said he didn't want to talk about it yet, so I said I'd make you tell me today."

"He still likes me?"

"Yea. He thinks you're a challenge. He likes the idea of chasing and claiming you. Just… don't push him away, Cam. I know you have some shit you're trying to work out… but you need to get that shit together before you miss out on a good nigga.

He's perfect for you. A gentleman with a savage ass attitude. Don't lose him because of a feeling. A feeling of fear. Let that shit go, cuz."

"You're right. Besides, if I go back home and tell my mama that I didn't keep my promise she gone chew my ass up."

"I already know. So get up, get cleaned up, and put on a dress that will make that nigga come running back to this room."

I just want You near Me

Rule was nervous for two reasons – his brother's nervous energy had transferred to him, and he was nervous about seeing Camryn.

When he left her last night he didn't plan on going back, but he couldn't leave things unresolved. After they cleared the air his heart was even heavier. He could tell she wanted him near... but he refused to break his own heart while trying to secure hers.

He could have understood her anger and fear had he been the one initiating the contact with Diana, but for her to have gone off her rocker because Diana was reaching out to him...

Rule understood that men and women were wired differently. Women were multitaskers and thinkers while men on the other hand were single focused.

The moment he set eyes on Camryn she became his focus and he was bound and determined to chase and pursue her until she approved and accepted him and all he had to offer.

She walked inside of the observation deck and reminded him of why he'd committed himself to pursuing her in the first place. Her long auburn hair was flat ironed for the first time since they'd met. She was wearing a sleeveless form fitting knee length red dress with a mid-thigh side split. Her red lips had him licking his in anticipation.

"I'll be back," he muttered to Power before walking towards her and meeting her halfway in the middle of the aisle.

"Hey," Camryn spoke softly.

"You look..." Rule took a step back and looked her up and down. "If you don't want me to walk around you turn around and let me see that ass."

"Rule," Camryn whispered as she blushed and took a step back.

He took a step forward.

"I ain't playing, Cam."

She met his eyes quickly then slowly gave him a full view of her.

Rule ran his hand down his jaws and bit his lip as he enjoyed his view. His physical attraction to her had never been a secret, but before he made love to her he wanted to be sure that she knew that she could trust him, feel safe with him, and feel cared for.

"You're beautiful, baby," he acknowledged as he ran his fingers through her hair. Resting his hand on her waist.

"Thanks. You look good. Really good."

Rule pulled her closer and licked his lips.

"Stop licking your lips at me," Camryn begged.

"Why?"

"Showing me them dimples. Those dimples and those freckles... just stop."

He chuckled and held her tighter.

"I can't help it, Camryn. Especially with you looking as good as you looking. You did this shit on purpose. You know red is my favorite color."

Camryn smiled with her lips and gray eyes, but both fell at the feel of his manhood growing against her.

"Rule…"

"Relax. I have self-control."

"But I can… feel it."

"Not yet you don't."

"Are you coming back tonight?"

"I don't know."

"Why not?" She whined.

Rule smiled and put some space between them.

"I don't want to make love to you tonight, Cam. We need to take this shit slow. You got some issues that we need to work out. I'm not going to commit to you while you're emotionally unavailable and try to change you.

We can kick it until you're ready… but I'm not setting myself up to be hurt. Having sex will just complicate this even more."

"Fine, we don't have to have sex. I just want you near me."

"I can't hold you tonight with your hair like this and not think about pulling it while I'm sliding in and out of you deeply from behind."

His hand wrapped around her hair and he pulled her into his chest.

"I need us to be on the same level emotionally and mentally first, baby," he continued as he watched her eyes close and her lips open. "I want you too bad right now because I know your little temper tantrum was only because you like me."

She opened her eyes and looked into his.

"You mean… that didn't push you away?"

"Hell nah. It's gone take more than that to push me away."

Camryn smiled softly and nodded.

"Okay. I respect that."

"Good. I'll spend the day with you of course… I'm just… not tryna put myself in the position to have to fight what I'm feeling if I don't have to."

"But you *don't* have to."

"Camryn…"

"I know. I know." Her smiled widened genuinely as she wrapped her arms around his waist. "I missed you. I missed your energy. Your presence."

"I missed you too." Rule cupped her cheeks inside of his hands and kissed her forehead. "I missed you too."

You will Never Stand Alone

After the wedding, Rule and Camryn said their goodbyes to Power and Elle and saw them off. Then they changed clothes and started their day together. They went sightseeing and took a helicopter ride. Next, they had dinner and headed back to the suite.

Midway into their conversation Rule received a phone call that completely changed his expression and mood when he returned to the suite. His clothes reeked of weed and his eyes had lowered and reddened. He sat across from Camryn and looked everywhere but at her.

"You... wanna talk about it?" She inquired.

He shook his head and met her eyes.

"Just some business shit. Niggas think since I'm out of town they can catch me slipping."

"Do you need to go back early?"

"Nah. Yancey is taking care of it. I don't want to talk about that shit, though."

"Well what do you want to talk about?"

Before their conversation was interrupted with his phone call they were talking about what was blocking their intimacy. Well, Rule was talking and Camryn was avoiding the truth.

"What we were talking about before I got that phone call."

Camryn rolled her eyes and inhaled deeply.

"Ion wanna talk about that," she mumbled.

"So you never wanna get the dick then is what you saying?"

She scratched her scalp and sat back in her seat.

"You're not playing fair."

"How not?"

"You can't arouse me and let me feel it and then deny me of it."

"I'm not denying you. I told you what had to happen before we took it there. So it's on you. You have the power in your hands, Camryn. Not me."

"Fine. I know that I've rebelled against my family pattern. In my rebellion I've... kept myself from experiencing romantic love to avoid hurt and rejection. I know I portray the stereotypical *strong woman I don't need a man* persona. I know relationships are where my deepest fears arise."

"What are you going to do with that knowledge?"

"I want to change, but you gotta understand... this defense mechanism has been up for years. Literally a decade. I haven't been in a real relationship since I was fourteen and that was some puppy love shit. Since then... I've dated niggas and fucked around... but I've never given a man access to my heart.

I want to trust you I promise I do... and really my fear has nothing to do with you. And I don't want to take it out on you..."

"Just..." Rule held up his hands and stopped her. "What's your biggest fear externally?"

"I'm scared of heights."

Rule looked her skeptically.

"You're scared of heights? We flew out here and rode I don't know how many roller coasters at the amusement park."

"Not that kind of heights. Like... me being in the air alone. Like... I could never skydive. If I'm in the literal air... that... I just can't. Planes and rides are cool because I'm not alone and I can close my eyes and not be aware of my surroundings. But like those bungee rides where you're just hanging in the air by two pieces of string. I can't do that."

"So if I would've hung you over the patio railing..."

"I would've shitted on myself."

Rule smiled and deepened his dimples causing her to smile.

"If I help you face that fear... will you let me help you with the other ones?"

Camryn leaned into the table.

"Why do you want to?"

"Because I want you. All of you. The *whole* you."

"Why?"

"Why not?"

"Rule..."

"I already told you why. When we went out for lunch. I told you if you genuinely accepted me for me and didn't want to change me you were going to be mine. You're beautiful. You have the spirit of a nurturer and lover... a seeker of life and truth... but you can't see the truth sitting right in front of you. I just can't understand that.

But I know you don't need me to understand you. You just need me to love you. The rest will work itself out."

"Rule, you can't say shit like that and not plan on following it up with letting me feel that love. I love sex. You might have great self-control but I don't."

He smiled and pushed his seat back from the table.

"Come here." It was when he used this low tone that she found herself completely captivated and under his spell. Camryn stood and walked over to him. Apprehension apparent in every step. Her shoulders were caved in and her head hung low.

"Sit on my lap."

Camryn straddled him and avoided his eyes until Rule lifted her head and forced her to look at him.

"This isn't helping," she said barely above a whisper into his lips before he covered hers with his.

"Why don't you ever have on panties?" Rule asked as he grabbed her ass.

"I don't like wearing clothes and feeling restricted. I like to let my body breathe and be free. If you weren't here I'd be walking around naked."

"Shit I ain't stopping you. How is it you want your body to be free but you trap your heart and mind?"

"Rule…"

"Is this closeness helping you?"

His hands went up her stomach and landed on her breasts. He squeezed and she moaned as her head flung back.

"Don't you want to be free, Camryn?"

"Yes," Camryn moaned as his tongue swirled across her neck. "You gotta stop," she pleaded.

"Are you gonna open to me?"

"Yes."

The vibration of his phone on her leg pulled Camryn from her trance. She looked down at his pocket as if she could see who was calling him.

"Ignore it," he said standing and tightening his grip around her waist.

"But it might be important."

"Nothing is more important to me right now than you."

She smiled as heat radiated from her skin.

"That was sweet."

"That's the truth." Rule laid her on the bed and pulled his shirt off. "No sex, Camryn."

"Then why are you getting naked?"

"I want us to be naked and unashamed. Completely exposed and vulnerable with one another. I want your skin on mine."

"Rule, I can't take that."

"You can and you will."

Rule pulled his phone from his pocket and sat it on the bedside table.

She licked her lips as he removed his pants and boxers. For a moment... he stood there... as if giving her time to take all of him in. All of him in. From his tatted and cross branded pecan skin to his pierced ears, deep dimples, and freckles.

Her eyes lowered and rested on the gift between his thighs. Immediately she began to cry between hers. His length. His width. His curve. She looked long enough to memorize the pink of his tip to the veins along his shaft before looking up and meeting his eyes.

He pulled the comforter back and slid under it.

"You gone lay with me?" Rule asked as she looked down at him. "You gone be free?"

Camryn grabbed the bottom of her shirt to pull it over her head but he stopped her.

"Unh unh. Get up and let me see it all."

She smiled that confident smile that he knew was always hidden within her and stood.

His eyes traveled down to her feet as she removed the shirt. By the time his eyes focused in on her center she'd taken it off.

"Are you fucking serious right now, Camryn? Fuck my life. Why didn't you warn me?"

Camryn chuckled and looked down at her body.

"What are you talking about?"

"You got your clit pierced. Now I wanna play with that shit. I know that's going to make you cum hard."

"You'd be the first to find out. I haven't had sex since I got it."

"Good. Get in."

Rule scooted slightly to the middle of the bed to give her space to climb inside. When she did she laid on top of him and closed her eyes in relief and pleasure.

"Your body is beautiful, Cam." His left hand fingered through her hair, the right squeezed her ass. "It's the perfect size for a nigga like me. Your ass fits perfectly into my hands. Your breasts. Your thighs. I can't wait to spread them thighs."

"Rule."

"I'm sorry."

"But thank you. Your body is uh… I'm scared of something else now. And you sexy as hell."

She didn't hear his laugh, but she felt his body shake.

"When the time comes I'll be gentle."

"But it's not tonight?"

"No, it's not tonight. No matter how much I want to play with that clit and taste it."

"Rule…"

"I'm sorry."

Camryn turned her back to him and they began to spoon.

"Tell me about your goals," she whispered as her eyes closed in relaxation.

"Awww shit! You mean we about to have a get to know you conversation and I didn't have to force it on you?"

"Get serious, baby."

"Awwww shit! Now I'm baby?"

"Rule!"

Camryn tried to sit up but Rule held her tighter.

"Alright, alright. I'm done. See what being free and opening up does? I'm just excited, Cam."

"Umhm. Just tell me."

She turned to face him and smiled at the sight of his. Camryn threw her leg around his body and he moaned as she closed her eyes and bit down on her lip.

"You might be right. Just the slight feel of you against my clit... that pressure... feels amazing already."

"I thought I had self-control... but that's fading away with you," he admitted before grabbing her thigh and putting her on her back. "I'm gonna go," he mumbled.

"Rule... you..."

Rule silenced her with a quick kiss then hopped out of the bed.

"But you don't have to leave. You can stay here. I wanna talk to you. You can't make me open up and then shut down on me."

He dropped his pants and looked up to the ceiling.

"Just talk to me... *please*." Her voice was softer as she grabbed his hand and pulled him back to the bed.

"Cam, I..."

"I get why we can't have sex and I agree with you. I want to explore you in ways that I've never experienced another man before. We'll get through this together."

"That's making it worse," Rule whined.

Camryn laughed and nestled herself in the middle of his chest.

"That's what you get for giving me such a hard time. Your ass ain't going nowhere tonight."

"Oh… so it's like that now? You locking a nigga down?"

"Absolutely."

"What took your ass so long?"

"I don't know. I've always been attracted to you. I just… was scared. But you're so patient with me. You make it easy to love you.

I mean… want to love you. Consider loving you. Not that I love you or want to love you. Not that you aren't lovable you are very… very lovable. God help me. This is why I don't talk."

"You don't want to love me? I want to love you."

Her body tensed against his but relaxed as he rubbed her back.

"You wanna love me?"

"I do."

Camryn lifted the top of her body from his and looked into his eyes. His fingers massaged her scalp as hers caressed his freckles.

"What are you doing to me?"

"Just what you need," Rule mumbled before pulling her face down to his and kissing her lips.

Camryn returned his kisses willingly before lifting her head and looking into his eyes. He smiled. She smiled.

"So you wanted to know my goals?" He asked finally.

She nodded and rolled over to the side of him.

"Well…" Rule continued pulling his arms up and his hands behind his head. "My vision is to be financially stable enough by the time I'm thirty to leave the streets and retire actually. I want to spend the rest of my days traveling and doing something positive with my time and money.

To keep my flow of income going I'll have a few residual streams of income going, but nothing that will require more than a couple of hours of my time a week. Some shit I'll be able to just sit back and collect checks for. Like… business investing or real estate investing. My goal is to be married with at least one child by then, but I want two total."

"What about school? Will you ever go back?"

He inhaled and exhaled deeply.

"Ion know. I would like to, but if I did it wouldn't be for Law. I'd rather go and be able to counsel people. I love analyzing people, problems, and situations and coming up with solutions. Especially young niggas. Before I die I want to start a nonprofit for young niggas.

A place where they can come and have fun without having to be in the streets. Somewhere they can learn trades and skills to avoid having to take that illegal route. I want to show them that they can make money the legal way. That the streets aren't the only option."

Camryn propped herself up on her elbow and looked down at him. He looked at her and smiled.

"What's stopping you, Rule? You have all these great ideas... all this positivity... this great mind and spirit... but you're wasting away in the streets. Why wait, baby? Why not start doing all that shit right fucking now?"

"What about you? What are your goals?"

Camryn shook her head and laid back down.

"By thirty I want to be done with Graduate school and working towards my Doctorate. I want to use my influence and position to be able to help young women love and respect themselves. Embrace their femininity and womanhood.

That's my passion. I already have permission to start an after school program when the schoolyear starts. I'm so excited."

"I can tell. Your eyes lit up and your smile was wider than I've ever seen."

Camryn bit down on her lip and looked towards the ceiling.

"Yea. That's what it's about for me. Leaving those prints on their minds and hearts. Having a positive impact on their lives."

"I'll consider it," he mumbled turning on his side.

She did the same. "You'll consider what?"

"Going back to school and starting on my nonprofit before I'm thirty."

Camryn smiled and kissed him quickly. "Good."

"You don't have any personal goals? No personal vision for your life? Marriage? Babies? Hell getting a boyfriend?"

She closed her eyes to avoid his. "No. Not really."

"Is that something that you don't want period? Look at me," Rule ordered softly as he cupped her cheek and stroked it with his thumb. "Because if it's not... there really is no point in me continuing my pursuit of you."

"I mean... I wanted that when I was younger..."

"But now?" Camryn shrugged and closed her eyes – trying to ignore the fear and hope in his. "Camryn..."

"I don't know, Rule. Can we just take this slow? I'm trying."

Rule nodded and removed his hand from her face.

"Yea. Sure. I ain't tryna rush you, but I ain't finna waste my time either."

"I respect and understand that."

"You need to communicate with me, Camryn. If we're not going to be on the same page, I can't invest in this. In us. I'm not for wasting time and energy, and I for damn sure ain't for wasting space in my heart."

"So I have to tell you now?"

"Nah, but damn... your mind ain't changed at all over the past few days? You mean you don't have an idea of whether or not that's something you want? Fuck in general... I'm talking about with me."

"I... I guess." Her voice was soft and low. So low he hardly heard her.

"Alright, Cam. We don't have to talk about it anymore," he mumbled getting out of bed.

"You leaving?"

"Yea. I'm getting sleepy so I'm gone head on out."

"But I thought you were staying?"

"I thought I was too. Really ain't no point now, though. That'll just make me get even more attached to your crazy confused inconsistent fine ass."

Camryn smiled bitterly as tears filled her eyes. Her pride. Her walls. Her stubbornness. Her fear. Were consuming her in ways she'd never noticed until she met Rule.

"Rule... I... I really don't want you to go," Camryn admitted as she put her feet on the carpeted floor.

Sitting on the edge of the bed she looked at him and tried her hardest to hold her tears in.

"I know my roots go deep. I know this shit goes deep. I know it's going to take more than a few days to pull up the roots but I want you to love this shit out of me, Rule."

"And I have no problem doing that, but would you be able to refill me? I'm not tryna be empty giving all of me to you for nothing in return. If you're not even willing to try..."

"I am." Her tears began to fall as she stood. "I am willing to try. But I just... need... some time. I can't... change overnight. I would if I could I've tried. I've tried to be like a normal woman. Wanting normal things. I've tried to see myself married with kids. I've tried, Rule... but the thought of that scares the life out of me."

"Does it? Is loving and losing what's really scaring you, Camryn? Or is that just an excuse to not try?"

"An excuse? Why would I not want to try?"

"You tell me. Didn't you say you were all for helping people reach their full potential? How can you help others reach their full potential and be whole when you aren't even doing it yourself? How can you preach being whole when you don't even practice that shit yourself?

That's the fucking problem! I'm tryna give your ass all of me and a whole love and you're half a woman. You can't accept me and what I'm trying to offer because you're not whole yourself. And you want me to settle for being half loved while giving you all of me? Nah. I can't."

"What the hell? Why are you doing this? Where is this coming from?"

"I'm sitting here trying to get you to open up but you just keep shutting down on me. I'm sick of this shit, Camryn. I'm the most patient impatient man in the world.

I'll give you all the time in the world to get your shit together if I think you're trying and willing but if I feel like you're wasting my time I have no time for it."

Camryn watched him dress and sat back down. Her heart smacked against her rib cage as if it was a wild gorilla trying to be loosed.

"I understand," she muttered as she wiped her face.

"I don't need you to understand, Camryn. I need you to prove to me that my heart isn't aching for you for no reason."

"Well I don't know why it is, Rule. I don't know why you want me. What have I done for you to like and want me besides be damaged?"

"That's... that's just it, mane. You ain't did shit. You don't *have* to do shit. I don't love because of anything somebody has done. **My love is unconditional. Your actions are irrelevant**.

Niggas got the game backwards. We try and force people to love us and receive our love like they owe us or some shit, but God don't even force His love on us. So who are we to try and force someone to be with us and love and accept us?

He lets us come to Him willingly because He loves us that much and He knows the value of what He has to offer. I know I'm a damn good nigga, Camryn. I know my love could change your life. I chose you. I chose you. Now it's up to you to accept me.

I ain't tryna make you fall in love with me. I'm tryna get you to rise in love with me. I ain't tryna make you fall and stumble. See..."

Rule dropped his shirt and walked over to her. He grabbed her by her shoulders and forced her to stand.

"Camryn, if you don't hear nothing else I say hear this and I swear this shit will change your life if you let these flowers grow in your mind. Let me water these flowers and watch them grow from your mind." His hands covered her cheeks. "Are you listening? Are you paying attention?"

She nodded and covered his wrists with her hands.

"I'm open. Teach me."

"Only immature people fall in love. They stumble. They can't stand. They can't manage. They get into a relationship and it consumes them. They lose themselves. They lose themselves because they aren't whole and they don't know how to stand alone."

Rule covered her heart with his hand. "But whole mature people… they know how to be and stand alone. When a whole person gives love they give it with no strings attached. They expect nothing in return. They are grateful for the opportunity to do what they were created to do… love. They feed you with all they have and you feed them with all you have and because you both are whole you never end up empty.

Because you're transferring love from one to another. Whole people help others with their love. They help them to be free. Your father and your step-father weren't whole. They weren't mature in love. Your mother couldn't have been either to allow them to do that to her.

Immature people who fall in love destroy each other. They take each other's freedom and energy. They feed off of each other… trying to make themselves whole and fill the holes in their souls… but it doesn't work.

They just end up stripping that person of all they are and then tossing them to the side as if they weren't enough. That's what they did to your mother.

Avoiding love is not how you break that cycle and avoid having to experience what your mother experienced. Becoming whole and mature is the only way to avoid that, Cam. That is the only way."

Rule wiped the tears from her cheeks and kissed her forehead.

"You are denying me of what I was created to do by not letting me love you, woman. Let me love you," he pleaded softly. "I ain't gone ask again or force my love on you. You need to make up your mind now. Is this what you want... or not?"

"Yes," she whispered with no hesitation as her arms wrapped around his waist.

"Say it."

"This is what I want. I want you."

"And you're committed to trying?"

"Yes, Rule."

"Then we can take things as slow as you need us to, but if I feel like you're not going to put in the effort..."

Camryn grabbed his neck and pulled his lips down to hers.

Rule seized her by her ass and pulled her into his body. Her arms wrapped around his neck as he lifted her and wrapped her legs around his waist. Her lips went from his lips to his cheek to his neck as he carried her to the bed. He dropped her onto it gently and took a step back.

"It's not the right time," he announced as he unzipped his pants.

"Then why are you taking your pants back off?"

"Because I want you to agree with me."

"And you think *that's* going to make me agree with you?"

"I want you to tell me it's too soon. That we need to wait."

"Fuck that."

"Camryn…"

"I want you. Right now."

Camryn watched him remove his clothing as if that was all he needed to hear. The soft buzz of his phone vibrated in the room. Her eyes went from his eyes to his pants that he tossed on the floor.

"Ignore it," he demanded.

This time, she didn't protest.

Rule crawled into the bed and between her legs and asked, "Are you sure?"

"I'm positive."

His lips covered hers as their suite phone began to ring.

"Who the fuck has the number to the suite?" He almost yelled, unable to mask his annoyance.

"I don't know. Nobody."

Rule groaned and reached for the phone on the bedside table.

"Yea?" He barked. Camryn watched as his face went from angry to calm and back to angry. "Are you fucking serious?"

Rule jumped from the bed as he continued to listen to the person on the other line. Camryn sat up and covered herself with the comforter.

"Aight. Fuck it. I'm about to step out and get up with Yancey. I wanted to take my baby out tomorrow but we gone have to cancel that shit and head back home early. This nigga needs to be stopped now."

Camryn got out of bed and started packing her things.

"Nah. I hear you, big bro, but that shit is unforgivable. That nigga trying me. He's testing my gangsta. He thinks since I'm the only one left in the business that I can't handle this shit by myself. He thinks I can't handle this shit without you and Pops. But I'm gone show his ass better than I can tell him. Ima get up with you when you get back home, though. Enjoy your wife."

Camryn heard who she now knew to be Power yelling through the phone as Rule disconnected the call. Rule put the palms of his hands on the table, closed his eyes, and took in a few deep breaths before turning to face Camryn.

"I'm sorry, but we gotta go early. I need to take care of some shit back home."

"That's... that's fine. Are you... this... I can't lose you, Rule."

The phone began to ring again. Neither of them acknowledged it.

"You won't. Don't get scared on me."

"I'm not. I'm just saying. I don't want to lose you."

He smiled softly and walked over to her.

"I got this. I'm not going there with you. I don't want you involved in that part of my life."

"But I need to know that you're going to be safe."

"I will be."

"Who's going to be with you? Can't this wait until Power gets back?"

"Nah. That's the problem. These niggas don't see me as nothing but Muhammad's baby boy and Power's little brother. Ever since I took over the business these niggas have been trying to scoop it from under me."

"Listen, I know you're upset right now... but just listen. These niggas know you're out of town, that's why they did whatever they did. If you go home with guns blazing, you could be walking into a trap. Just... wait.

Think this shit through and come up with a clear plan of attack. If you don't want to talk about it and let me help you fine. Just clear your mind and think logically first. Wait for Power. Or at least give them enough time to think you aren't going to do anything about it. And when they've gotten comfortable..."

"Smash on they asses," he interrupted, looking past her in deep thought. After a few seconds passed he returned his eyes to hers and smiled. "That's smart. I needed you for this. Had I been by myself I would have went home and walked straight into some shit I wasn't prepared for because of my anger. Thank you, baby."

He pulled her body closer to his.

"Although I don't want you to do anything I know I have no say in what you do. And I told you I would never try to change you. So the least I can do is help you and think for you when you can't think for yourself."

"I appreciate you for that. I swear I needed that shit. Thank you." Camryn nodded as he released her. "I need to get dressed and call Yancey."

"Do what you gotta do. I ain't going nowhere."

"Shit… after that… you bet not."

Camryn blushed and returned to the bed as the phone rang again.

"Can I answer?" She asked.

"Yea."

Rule grabbed his clothing and headed to the bathroom.

"Hello?"

"Cam, where's Rule?"

"He's in the bathroom."

"Listen, I need you to keep him from going home until I get there."

"No, no. No. That's not necessary. Stay where you are. I calmed him down. He's not leaving tonight."

The other end of the line grew quiet. Camryn pulled the phone from her ear and looked at it.

"Power?"

"Yea I'm here. I just can't believe that. Nobody can talk him down when he gets pissed. Especially not that soon. I was about to fly out there to go home with him because it ain't no telling what his ass was gone do."

"Yea. I don't know what's going on but I told him he needs to just take some time and think and wait for you. I don't know if he's going to wait, but he at least agreed to stay here and leave when we were scheduled to."

"Good. That's good. Thank you, Cam."

"You don't have to thank me for that."

"Yes I do. I won't go into detail because he obviously doesn't want you involved, but your quick thinking just saved my brother from walking into a trap. I'm grateful to you for that."

"It's nothing."

Rule walked out of the bathroom and she smiled.

"Is that Power?" He asked. She nodded. "Tell that mane I'm staying here tonight so he don't have to worry."

"I did. He was about to fly out here."

"Nah all that ain't necessary. I gotta learn how to stand alone now."

"Get back to Elle, Power. Everything is under control," Camryn said temporarily ignoring Rule's comment.

"Okay, cool. Y'all be safe. Tell him to call me before y'all fly out."

"Okay. You too."

Camryn hung up the phone walked over to Rule.

"You will never stand alone as long as you have me."

"With this I will."

"No. With nothing. I get that you're tough, and strong, and a man, and all that other good shit… but I got your back, Rule. On everything. I heard the hurt in your voice when you talked about your folks leaving the business. They may have left the business… but they didn't leave you."

Rule looked over her head and avoided her eyes.

"I hear you, Cam. Thank you."

"Do you really?"

She grabbed his face and forced him to look at her. His watery eyes made hers leak.

"I do," he mumbled as he hugged her waist.

"I got you, Rule. I promise I do."

"Then put on some clothes and come smoke a blunt with me."

Camryn pulled herself away from him and did as she was told – prepared to leave Las Vegas with a new goal.

At first, she was only concerned with herself. Her wants. Her needs. What she wanted to walk away from this with. Now… her main concern was being whatever and whoever Rule needed her to be to repay him for all he was quickly becoming for her.

You're Good for Me

Rule sat in his rental car and thought over their last day in Vegas before getting out to open her door. That afternoon they went skydiving and Camryn faced her biggest fear. Afterward they had lunch and headed for the airport. They still hadn't had sex and that was quite alright with Rule.

He enjoyed her companionship enough to be satisfied with just that.

They did, however, talk about sex – and that conversation intrigued him. He became intrigued with the fact that no man had ever made Camryn climax before. That was actually the reason why she had gotten her latest piercing. She was told that that would intensify her sexual experiences.

Rule opened his door, but Camryn's voice stopped him.

She questioned him about his next move.

The night before as they smoked he broke down and told her what was going on with his business. One of his workers, Marcel, tried to throw him under the bus and steal his clientele. Marcel took a couple of keys out of the delivery he was supposed to make to one of Rule's highest paying clients, Drake.

When Marcel approached Drake he told him that Rule had skimped him on the product and that he was starting his own business. Marcel offered to supply Drake with the same amount of product for half the price.

Drake told him that he would consider it, but immediately called Rule to make sure he knew what Marcel was up to. When he couldn't get in touch with Rule he called Yancey. Yancey was set to approach Marcel at the trap house Marcel was over, but before Yancey could reach the front door he was being shot at from all sides.

He called Power to see if he could get in touch with Rule to let him know that it was not only Marcel who had crossed them, but that he had multiple men from their payroll working with him.

Until they found out who it was they couldn't properly plan their attack. Camryn calming him down the night before helped him realize this, so Rule agreed to stand down until his mind was clear and he knew who else betrayed him.

"I'm just going to hold an emergency meeting with my camp to see if I can get some info from the ones that I know are loyal," he informed her.

"By yourself?"

"Yancey will be there. And I got a few niggas that I know I can trust."

Rule watched her face twist in apprehension, but she nodded and said, "Okay. Just be safe."

He smiled and stepped out of the car. Once Rule made it to her side of the car he opened the door and helped her out.

"I will be," he answered finally.

"Call me as soon as you leave."

"I'll do something better."

"What?"

"I'll come get you so you can spend the night with me."

Rule pushed her body towards the car with his and leaned against her.

"I would like that."

"Really? You not gone give me a hard time about getting attached to me and all that other bullshit you've been worried about?"

Her smile made him smile.

"No, Rule. I told you that I was going to try." She wrapped her arms around his neck. "I meant that shit."

He looked at her lips before taking them into his.

"Good."

As he grabbed her bags from the trunk he heard a door open and close.

"Hey, Ma," Camryn spoke.

Rule looked up and set eyes on an older version of Camryn and smiled genuinely.

"Hey, baby. I was just coming out to water your flowers, but since you're here you can do it."

"Flowers?" Rule asked.

"Yea. I have two gardens. A flower garden in the front and a vegetable garden in the back."

Camryn pointed to her mini garden as her mother walked back inside. "Bring your friend in too," she said before closing the door behind her.

"So you're into gardening? Why didn't you tell me that?"

She shrugged. "I don't know. I told you I don't like talking about myself. I love gardening though. I remember hearing a quote about the difference between a forest and a garden. Do you know?"

Rule looked from the garden to her skeptically. "What's the difference?"

"The things in a forest just grow. With no help from man. No structure. It just grows. But a garden is intentional. Everything planted is for a reason. You know what you want and you plant it. You sow the seeds that you want to reap.

A garden is in your control. It's something that you can nurture and prune and experience to your liking. After that I became fascinated with the idea of purpose and having control of something. Sowing just what I wanted to reap because life had given me things that…"

She cut her sentence off and looked at her garden.

With longing in her voice she continued. "I want to have a big house in the country with lots of farm animals too. I wanna be in my fifties selling fresh milk and eggs." That smile she had when she mentioned helping young women returned. "I want to have a couple of horses to ride too. I'm over the city life."

Camryn returned her eyes to his.

"Why didn't you tell me this when I asked about your personal goals? That's some shit we can make happen."

"I didn't think it mattered."

"Everything about you matters, Camryn."

Instead of arguing with him like he thought she would, Camryn pulled him into her by his shirt.

"Rule?"

"Yes, baby?"

"Thank you."

"For what?"

"For this trip. This experience. For caring about me and being interested in me. For wanting to cultivate me and make me better and help me grow."

He pulled one of her loose curls and lost himself in her gray eyes – wondering how she'd gone her whole life without a man doing all it took to make her his. And that's when he realized it was because God had been saving her for him.

"You don't have to thank me for that. I'm a man. I'm *your* man. That's what I'm supposed to do."

"You're my man?"

"Ain't I?"

"You really want to be?"

"Obviously."

She smiled and hugged him. "So… you're like… my boyfriend?"

He chuckled and pulled her from his chest to look into her eyes.

"Yea, if that's what you want."

"It is."

"Really?"

"Yes, Rule. I… you're good for me. I wanna be good for you too."

Rule licked his lips and pushed her back softly.

"Alright. Let me meet your Mama so I can leave before I spread them legs and see what that clit ring feel like."

You know I Love You... right?

While Camryn's mother questioned Rule Camryn sat back and smiled in disbelief. Her mother had never been interested in a man she had been dating before. She made a mental note to see what Elle told her mother when she returned from her honeymoon.

As the two talked, Rule was completely honest and upfront about his life and lifestyle. He had no problem telling her about his legal and illegal dealings. He told her about his childhood and the way his parents raised him. He told her about the vision he had for his life and the goals he had to make that vision a reality.

Her mother was pleased with how aware of himself and his wants and needs Rule was. She called him – a gentleman in the rough.

Although she didn't completely approve of his lifestyle she understood the reason behind it and respected the fact that it wasn't something he planned on doing forever. Brenda made Rule promise to protect and preserve Camryn and he agreed.

Afterwards he left to handle his business. Being sure to let Camryn know he would be back after he took care of it and stopped by his parents' home.

When he left, Camryn went to her room and started to unpack. Brenda leaned against the doorframe and watched her. When Camryn couldn't take her mother's prying eyes anymore she stopped and looked at her.

"Maim?"

"Be honest with me." Brenda walked into the room and sat at Camryn's desk. "Are you really into this boy... or did you do this just because I made you promise to have fun and enjoy yourself?"

Camryn leaned against her dresser.

When she began to really open up to Rule and enjoy his company she completely forgot about the promise she made to her mother.

She forgot about the fact that she wanted to prove that she could do without a man. Without love. That she could spend time with him and not get attached. In the course of a week Rule had completely reprogramed her heart and her desires. Camryn smiled sweetly and fluffed her curls.

"Ma... when I was with him... the promise that I made you wasn't even on my mind. He made me forget all about it. I really do like him."

"Good. I like him. He's good for you. He handles you. He deals with your stubbornness. He's patient with you. My only concern is... you know."

Camryn smiled and sat on her bed.

"He says he wants to be done by thirty."

"And how old is he now?"

"Twenty-six."

"So what is he going to do if he gets married before thirty? Have a wife and child involved in that lifestyle?"

"Well he doesn't want me involved, so I'm sure he wouldn't have his wife and children involved. Who knows… maybe he would leave. I don't know."

"You haven't asked him to leave?"

"Why would I ask him to leave? We just met. Who am I to make that demand on him? He has enough people trying to get him to leave. I don't want to add on to that number. I just… want to be here for him. That's it."

Brenda smiled and nodded. "And you trust him with your life and freedom?"

"I do. I know we just met… but I do."

"Okay. Well… if you trust him so will I, but if anything happens to you all hell is going to break loose. You're my only baby. I want you to experience love and all that comes with it, but not at the cost of your life and freedom, baby."

"I hear you, Ma."

"I guess I should tell you that your father called looking for you. They're having a family dinner for his youngest child Sunday before they head out for Disney World and he wants you to come."

Camryn's face firmed like stone. She hadn't spoken to her father in months and when she did speak to him it was casual conversation. She had never been to the home he shared with his wife. If he ever wanted to see Camryn, he came to her.

"Camryn, I said…"

"I heard you, Ma."

"Are you going to go?"

She smiled and shook her head as she stood and returned to her bags.

"You know I'm not going."

"Why not? Those are your siblings."

"Yea, they're my step-siblings… but that's not my family. I'm not gone fake like it is either."

"Yes they are, Camryn. Those kids have nothing to do with what happened between your father and I. You're their big sister. You used to love spending time with them. What happened?"

Camryn looked at her mother briefly before opening her closet and pulling her dirty clothes hamper out.

"Ask Victoria. Before she found out that I was spending as much time with them as I was I had the perfect relationship with them, but when she found out that he let me take them out and stuff she started tripping.

Then the next time I got them they were shut down. All quiet. They didn't want to do anything. It's like they didn't want to be around me. I know she told them some slick shit. They're just kids… so I didn't want to cause any trouble or make them feel uncomfortable.

If she doesn't want them around me that's fine with me. I grew up as an only child so I'm good. I got Elle. And they have each other."

"Well if she did say some slick shit then I'll handle that... but you can't take that out on the kids. They were crazy about you. Don't stop spending time with them just because their mother is a fool. I'll tell Edward about it."

"Don't waste your breath, Ma."

"Will you at least go to the dinner? For me? For the kids?"

"I'll think about it. I'm not making any promises, though. I might stay long enough to give Layla her gift. She's sweet as pie. I miss them I can't even lie.

Layla and Lonnie were my heart for a good little minute. I don't even know why he didn't tell her that I was spending time with them. He just fucks shit up for no reason with his lack of communication. I have no patience for that, Ma."

"I know, baby."

Brenda's soft voice and eyes softened Camryn's attitude.

"I'll go."

Brenda smiled. "Good girl. I'll let you unpack and unwind. Are you going out with Rule tonight or you staying here with your old lady?"

"Uh... I was going out with him, but if you want me to stay..."

Brenda quickly cut Camryn off. "Oh no, baby, go. Enjoy yourself. I'll be fine."

"Are you sure?"

"I'm positive."

"Okay."

Camryn waited until her mother left before she grabbed her phone and scrolled through her contacts. She stopped at Edward and stared at his name on her phone.

Truthfully, her uncaring and tough exposure only hid her true feelings – hurt and pain.

Being the only child her mother had, Camryn was overjoyed when she found out that Victoria was pregnant with Lonnie, but that quickly faded when Victoria made it clear that she wanted her children to have nothing to do with *urban* America.

Brenda checked her immediately, and Edward promised to talk some sense into her.

When Edward started to bring baby Lonnie over Camryn assumed Victoria had changed her mind. Over the years, Edward would come over and spend a few minutes with Camryn and leave Lonnie with her. Then it became Lonnie and Layla.

Sometimes their visits would last the entire time Edward had to work or run errands. Sometimes it would be for Saturdays when Edward was playing golf. But one Saturday Victoria fell ill. The kids were with Camryn and Edward told Victoria that they were well taken care of to soothe her mind. Victoria asked who her children were with and Edward told her Camryn.

Victoria became irate reinstating the fact that she told Edward that she didn't want her children around his black family without her being there to supervise them.

Ever since then Camryn made no effort to see her siblings or spend time with Edward for that matter. So she couldn't understand why he was inviting her over for dinner all of a sudden. Instead of thinking too deeply about it she decided to call him and see what he had to say.

"Camryn?" Edward asked as if he couldn't believe she'd returned his call.

"Yea. What's up?"

"How are you, honey?"

"I'm good. What's going on?"

"I was just trying to see if you would come over for dinner Sunday. We're having a family dinner for Layla bug's fifth birthday. I know that you two were... really close... and so I was trying to see if you wanted to come."

"When you say family dinner do you mean your family and your wife's family or just you and the kids?"

"Just Victoria and I and the kids."

"Oh. Well. I don't really want to be around her. I don't want my urbanness to offend her."

"Camryn, be mature."

"Why do I have to be mature? She's what? Twice my age? And I'm supposed to just let that slick shit fly out her mouth? I did when I was young and I let my mama handle that, but if she disrespects me I'm on her ass."

"Camryn, please. Victoria has matured herself over the years. It was her idea to invite you actually. She wanted to call and ask you... but she didn't think you would talk to her. Will you come over and give it a chance? Please?"

Camryn scratched her scalp and sighed into the phone.

"Fine. I'll stop by for a few."

"That's... I'll accept that. Dinner will be served at six."

"Cool."

"Bye, honey. You know I love you, right, Camryn?"

"Aight."

Camryn disconnected the call, laid back on her bed, and resisted the urge to call Rule. If he was in the middle of his meeting she didn't want to interrupt him with her issues. But as crazy as she was feeling as she turned over on her side she was willing to take that chance. She closed her eyes as a tear slid down her eye and nose.

"Ma!" She called out.

Seconds later her mother was crawling into her bed and taking her into her arms.

Tonight

Immediately after Rule's meeting adjourned he went to visit his parents, home to change clothes, and back to Camryn's place. The second she opened the door and checked him out from head to toe she pulled him into her and showed him how much she appreciated his presence.

Rule was dressed in a navy blue blazer with a gray fine checkered print. Underneath he sported a white frame fitting button down shirt. His charcoal gray slacks were custom made and they wrapped around his toned thighs perfectly.

But what set his look off was the pair of small thin glasses that adorned his face. This was the first time she'd seen him wearing glasses and they gave him a sexy educated grown man look that she had no problem vocalizing that she loved.

Between that, his freckles and dimples, and his pierced ears… she had been begging him to take her back to his place since they left hers, but Rule wanted to take her out and show her off.

And the outfit she had on was one that caused all eyes to be on her. She was dressed in a sleeveless and backless navy asymmetrical dress that hugged her hips perfectly. Her hair was pulled up into a bun and her face was lightly made with a matte velvet dark blueish black lipstick.

From the moment they walked into Privé, Rule had been struggling to contain his possessiveness.

He knew he had no control over the men's stares at his lady... but he refused to put up with any form of disrespect. His arm wrapped around her hips and he pulled her closer to him as he stared every onlooker in their eyes.

Camryn rubbed her hand against his six pack and looked at the side of his face. With her heels on they were the same height.

"What's wrong, baby?" She asked as he looked at her briefly before returning his attention to one man who had been looking extremely hard.

"You don't see all these niggas looking at you?"

Her soft chuckle caused him to release her and turn slightly to face her.

"Why would I be paying them any attention when I'm here with you?"

He blushed then hid it by licking his lips.

"You tryna sweet talk me?"

"I'm just telling the truth. But I understand. I see all these bitches looking at you."

Rule looked around uncertainly. "Who?"

"Nigga... all these bitches in this waiting area been looking you up and down."

"I didn't notice. I was too busy making sure these niggas knew you were mine."

Camryn smiled and wrapped her arms around his waist. He did the same to her.

"Have I told you how handsome you are?"

His lips grazed hers quickly before he replied.

"Like… seven times since I picked you up. Have I told you how beautiful you are?"

"Like… ten times since you picked me up. I see you tryna jock my style with this blue too."

Rule pushed her away playfully.

"Girl, please. You jocking my style."

"Whatever, nigga. You do look good though."

"You gone give me some pussy tonight?"

"Rule, you can't ask for it like that for our first time."

"Why not? You was throwing it at me in Vegas."

"Well… that was then. I want our first time to be special like you wanted it to be."

He groaned and ran his pointing finger down her neck.

"Fine. Can I at least taste it tonight?"

"Nope. I don't trust you."

His chuckle made her smile.

"What you mean? That's all I'm gone do. I give you my word."

"I hear you. But that wouldn't be all I would want you to do. So we need to just wait."

"Damn, mane. I should've took it in Vegas."

"Owens... party of two," the hostess called out.

Rule grabbed her hand and they followed the hostess to their table – until Camryn's free hand was grabbed.

"The fuck?" Camryn asked as she turned to see who grabbed her.

"I thought that was you," he spoke.

Rule stopped walking and turned to face them. His hand covered the man's and removed it from Camryn's immediately.

"Who the fuck is this nigga?" Rule asked Camryn.

Sensing Rule's temper he took a step back.

"This nigga I used to talk to. Derrick."

Derrick cleared his throat before speaking. "I ain't mean no disrespect. I just wanted to speak. Haven't seen you in a while."

"You can speak without putting your hands on my lady. Really... don't even speak. When she with me and when she ain't."

Derrick's face tensed up and Rule took a step towards him, but Camryn stopped him with her body.

"Chill out. Let's go," she mumbled into his lips before kissing them quickly.

Rule looked to the side of her at Derrick once more as he squeezed her ass, then grabbed her hand and continued his walk to their table.

When they were away from Derrick Camryn asked, "Really, Rule?"

"What?" Rule asked unaware as he pulled her seat back.

"Is that how you're going to react every time a nigga speaks to me?"

"Nah. That nigga put his hands on you. That was disrespectful. He could've just nodded at me first out of respect and then spoke to you. It ain't no reason for a nigga to be speaking to you while you with me anyway."

Camryn shook her head with a smile as she picked up the menu.

"You're a mess, baby. I love it though."

"Whatever. Ima need you to text all your little boyfriends tonight and let them know you got a man now and he ain't all the way there in the head, so if they see you out stay in their lane."

Her giggle softened his demeanor a little, but he was still irritated. If there was one reputation the Owens' men had in Memphis... it was that they tolerated no form of disrespect from anyone. Nor did they allow anyone to move in on their territory. Professionally and personally.

"Are you serious?"

"Dead fucking serious."

"Okay. I will. Come give me a kiss. That shit turned me on."

Rule stood and made his way to Camryn. After kissing her he asked into her lips, "So... I still can't get the pussy tonight?"

You can't Leave Me

When Camryn woke up the next morning… she was convinced she was hearing things.

Ignoring the sound of multiple animals ringing in her ears, she turned to the opposite side and tried to drift back into her sleep. When the sounds continued she opened her eyes and gave herself time to remember where she was before sitting up in Rule's bed. Camryn scratched her scalp and looked around before placing her feet on the floor and inhaling deeply.

Slowly she stood and slithered into his bathroom. A quick shower later and she was heading down his hallway in his t-shirt and a pair of sweats and Nike sandals. The sounds grew louder and louder as she neared his living room.

"Rule!" She called out as she continued to his kitchen.

He didn't answer. Camryn looked around the empty kitchen and sighed. The back door opened and closed and the sounds were loud enough to be coming from outside.

"What the hell?"

Camryn walked to his living room and found him smiling with a rabbit in his arms. She stopped walking abruptly and stared at the rabbit.

"Good morning, sleepy head. It's about time you woke up," Rule spoke as he walked towards her.

"Where did that come from?" She asked softly.

"Go outside and see." Camryn shook her head no as tears filled her eyes. "You want to hold her?"

"Rule, what did you do?"

Rule handed Camryn the rabbit and took a step back.

"I got a traveling petting zoo to come out. You did say you wanted a farm one day right?" She nodded as her tears fell. "Well... I figured this could be a taste of what you have to look forward to. They brought calves, rabbits, pigs, donkeys, horses, ducks... shit some shit I ain't never even seen before."

"Really?"

"Yea, go look. Go enjoy yourself."

"Why, Rule?"

"I just told you why. Now gone."

Camryn stood on her tip toes and kissed him.

"Thank you. This is the sweetest and most thoughtful thing anyone has ever done for me. I can't believe you did this. I'm so... I'm so... happy."

"You will be even more happy when you go out there. Usually they go to kid's birthday parties so they got you some cake and ice cream out there and a t-shirt. I'm gone grab my phone to take some pictures and I'll meet you out there."

Rule tried to walk away, but her hand on his forearm stopped him. Camryn opened her mouth... but closed it and shook her head. Rule pulled her into him, careful not to squeeze the rabbit.

"It's okay," he assured her.

"Rule, you can't leave me. You can't do shit like this for me and then leave me. You can't play with my emotions like that. If you're not going to stick around…"

"I ain't going nowhere crazy ass lil girl. Just accept me and what I'm giving you and enjoy me. Don't think about me leaving because I'm not, baby. I'm here. Now gone."

Camryn nodded and sluggishly walked outside. Her emotions overwhelmed her the minute she stepped on the back porch and took in the sight before her.

Animals of all kinds were walking around the backyard. An older lady walked over to her with a smile.

"Well hi, young lady. My name is Carla. I see you've met Rudy. Who would you like to meet next?"

Camryn looked from Carla to the calves.

"Can I… can I go pet the calves?" She asked with an innocence in her voice that made Carla smile harder.

"You sure can. Here… give me Rudy and go on over. We've got a newborn calf over there that you can bottle feed if you'd like."

Camryn's mouth opened as excitement covered her face. "Really? Oh my God!" She squealed.

Camryn walked over to the calves and stood next to a younger girl.

"Are you Camryn?" She asked.

"Yes."

"I'm Amy. It's nice to meet you."

"You as well."

"You wanna feed baby Porgy?"

"Yes."

Amy pointed to a nearby stool for Camryn to sit on. Once Camryn was seated Amy walked Porgy over to her lap. She handed Camryn the bottle and Porgy willingly accepted. As Camryn fed Porgy she ran her free hand along her coat with a sense of pleasure she'd never experienced before.

Her mind went to Rule and she looked for him. She found him a few feet away with his phone in his hand. She smiled and blinked tears away as her thoughts consumed her.

Was this love? Was this what she had been avoiding all of her life? Was this something that she could expect for the rest of her life? And if so... she was determined to find ways to give him everything he gave her back in return.

Simply Beautiful

Rule was in his living room waiting for Camryn to put together her surprise for him. He told her that she didn't have to do anything special for him but she insisted. So, he played his baby grand piano as he waited for her.

The creaking of his wooden floors gained his attention. His floors, ceilings, and main room walls were wooden. He had huge glass windows and multiple hanging lights pulling in natural sunlight when it was out.

Camryn walked over to him dressed in his favorite thing to see her in – his t-shirt. She sat next to him and he gripped her thigh and caressed it with his thumb.

"Can you play?"

Her fingers stroked the keys. "Nah. I can sing a little."

"Is that so?"

Rule stood and grabbed his guitar.

"That don't mean I want to. I'm shy."

"Fuck all that. I wanna hear you."

He began to play *Simply Beautiful*, one of his favorite songs by Al Green, and smiled as her eyes closed in euphoria. Her lips curved into a small satisfied smile as she swayed her head to his playing.

"If I gave you my love I tell you what I'd do… I'd expect a whole lot of love out of you. You gotta be good to me. I'm gonna be good to you. There's a whole lot of things you and I could do."

Rule stopped playing. She stopped singing and opened her eyes.

"You can sing," he mumbled in disbelief.

She smiled and stood, extending her arm towards him.

"Camryn… you can sing."

He stood and placed his hand inside of hers.

"I can do a lot of things, baby. Just explore me."

He entered his bedroom and smiled at the sight before him. When Camryn left a couple of hours earlier and returned she wouldn't allow him to see what she brought back… and now that he saw it… he couldn't believe it.

Rule was used to doing sweet and romantic things for women. He wasn't used to them doing sweet and romantic things for him.

She'd placed rose petals all across the floor. In the middle of the bed they were shaped into a heart. Candles and incense were blazing on his dressers and tables. His Beats pill had Al Green flowing lowly in the background. On his bedside table she had white chocolate covered fruit and massage oil.

"Do you like it?" She whispered as his arm wrapped around her waist.

He pulled her closer to his side and let out a loud breath.

"I love it. Thank you, baby."

Camryn stood in front of him and removed his clothing piece by piece. When he was nude she led him to the bathroom and cut on the shower.

"Take a shower and unwind. I'll be waiting for you."

She pecked his lips and returned to his bedroom.

For a moment... he just stood there. His heart... suddenly filled with unease. All this time... he'd spent his time trying to convince her that he wouldn't leave or hurt her, but he'd never really taken the time to consider how he would feel if she did that to him.

The closer they grew and the more she opened up to him, it felt as if he was taking the fear from her heart and harboring it inside of his. Running his hands down his face Rule stepped into the shower and tried to wash the thoughts from his mind.

I Ain't going Nowhere

Camryn didn't realize she'd fallen asleep until Rule's hand around her ankle woke her up. Gently he grabbed the other and pulled her legs apart. She opened her eyes and met his with a smile.

His fingers glided along her legs until they made their way between her thighs. Rule carefully removed the ring from her piercing.

"What are you doing?" She asked as he sat it on his bedside table.

"Making sure you know I'm making this pussy cum and not that damn ring."

She smiled but her smile quickly faded when his hands slid under her shirt. Sure, he'd touched her body before. He'd seen her naked before. But this time... this time was different. This time was leading to the first time.

Her heart began to flutter as he pulled the shirt from over her head and caressed her breasts before squeezing them softly.

Rule's body covered hers and he kissed along her neck and cheek, causing her chest to rise and fall rapidly. He stopped and looked down at her.

"I'm sorry. Do you want to wait?"

The concern in his voice made her throb and cry between her thighs. Biting down on her lip she shook her head no as she traced the freckles along his cheeks.

Rule covered her heart with his hand and she closed her eyes. After a few deep breaths the beating of her heart slowed down. She opened her eyes in time enough to catch him lowering his face to hers for a kiss.

A deep kiss. A passionate kiss. A full kiss. A wet kiss. A hard kiss. A soft kiss. A slow kiss.

He pulled his lips from hers and she whimpered.

"Loose your hair," he commanded before circling her nipples with his tongue.

Her back arched immediately as his hands clutched her thighs. After doing as she was told, Camryn moaned quietly as his lips kissed down her stomach. Up and down her thighs. As his hands spread her bottom set of lips and his mouth seized her clit.

His hands grabbed her waist as he used just his tongue to pleasure her most sensitive place. The clitoris is said to have at least eight thousand sensory nerve endings and Rule's tongue was hitting each and every one. Between his licking and sucking she felt her legs trembling and her walls pulsing.

Sensing she was on the verge of her climax Rule inserted one finger inside of her and massaged her G spot until she came and experienced her first orgasm. He lifted himself from her and wiped her cream from his mouth and chin.

She covered her face with her hands and rebuked her tears to keep them from falling. This was not supposed to happen. This was not supposed to get this deep. This was not supposed to feel this good. This real. This necessary. This normal.

His hands covered her wrists and he removed them from her face. Her smile was small as he kissed her tears from her cheeks.

"I ain't going nowhere," he whispered into her lips as he positioned himself at her center. "Do you believe me?"

"Yesss," Camryn moaned as he slid inside of her.

With two handfuls of her hair Rule pushed himself deep inside of her as she latched on to him.

"Fuck," he muttered pulling himself completely out of her – then entering her deeply again.

"Yes, yes, yes..." she whispered into his neck as he repeated this motion over and over again.

His tongue entered her mouth while he used the tip of his manhood to stroke her G-spot. She kissed him until she felt her walls tighten against him. Until they pulsed. Until her legs trembled. Until her body lifted from the bed. Until her lips quivered. Until moans erupted from deep within her.

"Ohhh shit, Rule," she moaned as he filled her with all of him.

Her nails went into his skin as he moaned and bit down on her neck.

"Okay," he muttered pulling her hair. "That's enough. Stop squeezing my dick before you make me cum," Rule pleaded.

"I can't help it," she whined as she felt herself gripping him tighter and tighter.

Camryn wrapped her legs around his waist as he buried his head in the pillow. Her orgasm subsided… but the tightness remained. The heat remained. The tingling remained. And a few deep and slow strokes later she felt her walls contracting yet again.

"Rule…" she moaned. "It… I… you keep… I'm about to… ohhh…"

He pulled out of her completely and watched her orgasm overtake her.

When her body became still he ordered her to, "Turn around."

Rule arched her back and entered her methodically and slowly. She moaned and buried her face in the middle of the pillow. That didn't last long. His right hand dug into her waist while his left pulled her hair.

"Yesss," she whispered gripping the sheets.

"Umhm," he moaned holding her tighter.

The smacking of his body against hers. The gushing of her juices out of her and on to him. His grunts and unwilling moans. All pieces of a puzzle that had her toes curling and her eyes rolling into the back of her head as he introduced her to her body in ways she'd never imagined before.

When it felt as if her insides opened even wider from his length she pulled her hand back and gripped his thigh. He chuckled and pushed her hand away as he continued to plunge deeply inside of her.

"Take this dick. This what you been wanting, right?" Her moan was her reply. Camryn lifted herself from the bed slightly and began to match his strokes. "Nu unh. Stop before you make me cum."

Rule released her hair and used both hands to hold her waist and control her movements. Camryn continued to throw her body onto his. The friction sent her into her fourth orgasm. His moans and hands wrapping around her neck made her cum harder. Weakly she fell into the bed with him right on top of her. And in just a few seconds they both drifted off to sleep.

You Know I got You

Sunday came quicker than Camryn wanted it to. Initially, she backed out, but Rule convinced her to go. Now they were sitting outside of Edward's home in Rule's car. Rule looked over at Camryn and she looked out of the window to avoid his eyes.

"Baby… how long we gone sit out here? I'm hungry. And I know we gone have to go somewhere else to get something to eat when we leave here because they probably gone be serving some shit I don't even want."

Camryn looked at him and smiled at the sight of his.

"I'm scared."

"Fear is an emotion. You were created to have dominion over all things. Don't let something intangible give birth to tangible actions. Control your emotions. Don't let that shit bring you out of yourself."

"But what if she says something crazy and I beat her ass?"

Rule chuckled and unbuckled his seatbelt.

"I'm not gone let you do that, Camryn. What I just say? *You* have to control your emotions. Don't let her get a rise out of you. If she says some disrespectful shit we can leave."

She nodded and almost whispered, "Fine. I'm ready."

Camryn waited until Rule opened her door and they slowly made their way up Edward's driveway. Her arm wrapped around Rule's and he looked down at her as he entangled his fingers with hers.

"You okay?"

She looked up at him and nodded. "I'm fine. Thanks for coming with me."

"You know I got you."

"Gimme kiss."

Rule smiled as he took her face into his hands and kissed her sweetly. His hands traveled down her back and stopped at her ass – pulling her into his chest.

Camryn rested her hands on his chest briefly before wrapping them around his neck. She moaned and he pulled away from her.

"Alright now. If you don't want me to take you back to the car and spread them legs, you need to cut all that moaning out."

"I can't help it, Rule. I can't get enough of you. You got me sprung now."

Camryn pushed his hands from her waist and rang the doorbell. His hand moved to her ass and he squeezed it with enough pressure to make her grip the doorframe for support.

"Stop. You can't tell me to stop and you do shit like that."

"Mane... let me."

"Un unh," she protested as she removed his hand.

"Aight. I got you faded."

"And what does that mean?"

"I'm gone remember that tonight when we get home."

Camryn's smile widened. "Rule, I'm not coming back tonight."

"Why not?"

"Because I don't want to be there every night."

"Why not?"

Edward opened the door and cut Camryn's reply off. He looked from Camryn to Rule before opening the door wide enough for them to enter.

"Hey, honey. Who's your friend?"

"I'm her boyfriend Rule. Pleasure to meet you," Rule spoke as he extended his hand.

Edward smiled and put his hand into Rule's.

"The pleasure is all mine. Come in and make yourselves comfortable."

Camryn stepped in and tears immediately filled her eyes. She scratched the back of her neck and turned to face Edward.

"Which way should we go? I've... never... been here before."

Edward's smile faded as he hid his hands in his pockets.

"Um... down the entry hall and to the right."

She nodded and took a few steps before stopping – causing Rule to bump into her from behind. His arm wrapped around her instinctively and he whispered into her ear.

"I got you. Don't you cry. You gone make me cry. And if I cry I'm fucking somebody up."

Her giggle made him release her.

"Rule can you go ahead in and let me talk to her for a second?" Edward asked walking towards them.

Rule looked at Camryn for permission to leave.

"I don't want you to go," she muttered grabbing his hand. "But... go."

"Are you sure?"

"Yes."

"Okay. Call me if you need me, Camryn."

Rule looked Edward over before walking in the direction he told them to go.

Camryn leaned against the wall and cupped her hands together.

"I'm sure... there's probably a lot you want to say... to ask. I'm sorry. You should have been invited over long before now. It's just Victoria..."

"It's cool. I get it. She's your wife. She comes first."

"Well, yea, but I should have told her that you were my daughter and you had just as much of a right to be here as Lonnie and Layla."

"You know what? That doesn't even bother me. I don't care about her not liking me. Honestly, I understand why she doesn't. I'm the product of your greatest desire and fascination – my mother.

You wanted a black queen and you had her. You just weren't strong enough to stick around. Just like I know that she knows that too. That's why she doesn't like me.

But what I can't understand is why we weren't good enough for you? Why did you just up and leave? I get that you didn't want to be with my mother anymore but damn why did you have to leave me too? It took years for you to actually start coming back around... and when you finally did you only stayed for a couple of minutes. What did I do to deserve that?"

"Nothing, honey. Absolutely nothing. Me leaving had nothing to do with you or your mother frankly. You're right... she *was* my desire. I craved your mother. I craved the melanin in her skin. Her curves. The power in her voice. The strength in her walk. I was obsessed with her.

And when she finally gave herself to me... I couldn't handle it. I was young then, honey. I couldn't handle the pressure of being a father let alone the pressure of being with someone of a different race. Having to hear complaints from both sides of the family... I ran.

But that had nothing to do with your worth or your mother's. That was a reflection of my character."

Edward grabbed her hand and pulled her closer to the front door. He looked down the hall before continuing.

"Your mother... she was... everything to me, Camryn. And you... you are my greatest creation. I just... allowed my fear to lead me and once I planted those seeds I felt like it was too late. Too late to make things right with either of you. So I got with Vickie and had Lonnie and Layla and tried to just... move on."

"Have you told any of this to my mother?"

"No. I couldn't. I can't."

"Why not? That would help her a lot. It's helped me already."

He smiled and looked away from her.

"I'm still in love with her, Camryn. I never wanted to let her go. I was just... scared. Then she got with Anthony and he screwed her over even worse than I did. I blamed myself for that because I left her. I just... figured she'd be better off without me."

"Do you even love your wife?"

"Of course I do. I've grown to love and appreciate her. I... tried to be a better man for her than I was your mother. That's why I've tried to respect her wishes as much as I have... but I'll never love her the way I love your mother.

My time with her...was... I just don't want you to think I don't care about you. Or that I don't love you. I know I haven't been the most present father, but I don't want that to shape you and turn you into..."

Camryn laughed quietly and took a step back. "My mother?"

Edward nodded. "She... told me about how you've been living when I was trying to get in touch with you. That's why I was so surprised to see you with a young man. Honey, that's no way to live.

I know I'm the last person to try and give you advice on love and relationships, so I'm not even going to try to, but I will say learn from my mistakes. We're motivated always by fear or love. My life is what happens when you're led by fear. If you don't want that to happen to you... don't be like me."

She ran her sweaty palms down her jeans.

"I still think you should talk to her. At least for closure so you won't continue to drag this around with you."

"On one condition."

"What's that?"

"That you come around more often."

"It's not going to happen overnight... me and your wife... but... I'll see what I can do."

"I'll accept that. Thank you, honey."

Camryn nodded and smiled softly before following him to the kitchen.

Love Yourself

Power and Elle were back from their honeymoon and Elle convinced Camryn to host a self-love workshop to start off her summer dance camp. She usually held it a month before school started but her trip to Vegas pushed it back. When they returned her first order of business was gathering her girls up the following Monday at her studio.

Camryn waited until Elle finished introducing her before she stood and walked to the center of the room. When she planned for the event she had a full speech prepared but after spending time with Rule her views of love and relationships were changing.

Instead of teaching them to completely throw themselves into their purpose and goals and ignore their need for companionship as she planned on doing she decided to be completely transparent with them.

"You guys…" she started before looking at Elle and shaking her head in reluctance. "I… I had this whole speech planned, right? I had all these ideas and activities… but none of that matters now. Now that I've truly began to practice what I preach. How many of you genuinely love yourselves?"

She watched as a few of them raised their hands immediately while others hesitated. Her eyes landed on a young girl whose skin was the same shade as hers. Their hair was the same texture. And her eyes were gray as well.

"Gray eyes… come here."

Slowly the young lady stood and made her way next to Camryn.

"What's your name, baby?" Camryn asked as she turned to face her.

"Braille."

"Braille? That's different. Is there a meaning behind it?"

"Um, my mom named me that because she said the love she and my father share is blind. She's black and he's white."

Camryn's heart dropped as she took a step back.

"Why did it take you so long to raise your hand, Braille?"

Braille shrugged and wrapped her arms around her stomach. "I… I don't know."

"Do you know what it means to love yourself? Do you actively practice self-love?"

Braille shook her head no and lowered her eyes. "I don't think so. I mean… I love me I'm sure. I don't know."

"Okay um… have a seat in the front over here and I'm going to go over seven habits that people who love themselves practice and if you don't do these things we're going to talk about how you can implement them in your life, okay?"

Camryn looked at Elle as Braille sat down and Elle clutched her heart in compassion. Grace immediately came to Camryn's mind. She was still in San Francisco. Her parents had yet to reach out to her and it ate at Elle on a daily basis.

"People who love themselves are aware of themselves. They know what they need. What they want. What they don't want. They know their goals and their purpose in life. They are focused.

Once they know what they want and need they are focused on those things and doing what it takes to make them happen.

They take care of themselves physically, mentally, and emotionally. They are able to set clear boundaries for their lives and their relationships. They know how to say no to things that aren't good for them. Relationships that aren't good for them. They surround themselves with positive people.

They don't hang around with people who bring negative energy into their lives or hinder them in any way. They forgive themselves when they've done wrong. They don't allow themselves to be led by fear or guilt."

She inhaled deeply and smiled softly. "All six of these things allow them to live intentionally. They allow them to pursue their purpose. That's what I was going to emphasize to you guys today… but I think we need to start from the beginning.

So number one to love yourself you must be aware of yourself. You have to know yourself. Number two you have to be focused. Number three you have to take care of yourself. You can't love others if you don't properly love yourself, nor can you care for others if you don't properly care for yourself.

Number four you have to have clear boundaries. Don't be a sucker. Don't be a pushover. Don't let this lil niggas talk you into doing anything that you know you shouldn't be doing just because they're some little horn dogs. Don't let these lil fast tail girls have y'all doing some shi- stuff y'all know is wrong because of peer pressure.

Number five you have to surround yourself with positive people. Number six you have to live fearlessly with no regrets. No fear. And should you fail you have to forgive yourself. Number seven you have to live intentionally.

Now… how many of you do five or more of those things on a daily basis?"

No one raised a hand.

"Okay, how many of you do at least three of those things on a daily basis?"

A few raised their hands. Camryn smiled.

"Okay. I want you all to stand up and grab those notebooks beside Elle. We're going to chop each of these things down and I'm going to tell you how you can implement each habit into your every day routine. Life is about relationships, ladies. Whether we want to admit it or not we were created to commune with God and then others. We were created to love and have relationships.

First we must work on our relationship with God. Then our relationship with ourselves. Then our relationship with others. Think about a triangle."

Camryn walked over to the wall and floor length mirror and drew a triangle with lipstick. At the top she wrote God. At the left point she wrote self. At the right point she wrote others.

When the girls were seated again she walked back over to them.

"Most times we don't take the necessary steps to love ourselves because we worry about being conceited… or we're just so focused on our relationships with others that it just… doesn't seem like a factor to us.

But you cannot really love and respect others until you love and respect yourself. Now I'm not talking about this worldly selfish artificial love I'm sure you guys have grown up learning about. I'm talking about unconditional selfless love that's based on actions not feelings.

Actions are what should *lead* to feelings. Feelings should never be the foundation for your relationship because feelings change.

I want you all to draw a triangle in the middle of your paper just as I did on the mirror. When everyone is done we'll take it from there."

Camryn walked over to Elle and Elle grabbed her wrist and pulled her to the side.

"Grace," she mumbled as tears filled her eyes.

"When was the last time you talked to her?" Camryn asked.

"A week ago. She's been working and going to school. She seems happy but I'm still not okay with her being there with him."

"I feel you. You and Power should go and see her."

"I'm going to talk to him about it. What do you think about Braille? I swear she reminds me of a young you."

"I know right. I'm going to chat with her one on one and see what's up with her."

"Good. Gone on so we can go to lunch after this. I'm hungry."

"Fine. Greedy ass."

He's Perfect

Camryn and Elle went to Café Eclectic for lunch when the workshop was over. As they waited for their food they snacked on nachos. Elle ordered a patty melt while Camryn ordered their signature devil's pie – a bowl of mac n cheese mixed with spicy diablo chicken topped with crust.

Camryn leaned into the table and put both elbows on top of it.

"Okay… I've been waiting to see you face to face to hear about the honeymoon. Was it great?"

A smile covered Elle's face immediately.

"Camryn… it was everything. I love that man so much. More than words can say."

"Did you guys do any sightseeing or did you lock yourselves in your room the entire time?"

"We took in some sights our last two days there, but I want to hear about you and Rule. What happened when we left?"

Camryn sat back in her seat and smiled just as widely as Elle.

"We… talked. He broke down all my walls, Elle, and I promise I didn't make it easy."

"So are you guys like in a committed relationship now?"

Camryn nodded and took a sip of her lemonade.

"Yea. When we came back he rented a fucking traveling petting zoo for me, Elle. Who even does that shit?"

"Are you serious? You told him about wanting to have a farm one day?"

"Yeap. When he dropped me off and saw my garden. That's not it, though."

Camryn looked around the restaurant and leaned deeper into the table. Elle did the same.

"We... I let him..."

"Y'all fucked?"

"Girl. That nigga made love to me then he fucked me. My ass cried and everything."

Elle chuckled and shook her head as she stood and pushed her chair closer to Camryn's.

"Why did you cry, Cam?"

Camryn released a hard breath and shook her head.

"I guess I was just caught up in the beauty of the moment. You know I love sex, but no man had ever made me cum before. Like... the journeys have been great but I've never reached that destination.

In some kind of twisted way, I felt like God was punishing me for not waiting until I was married. I figured I would experience that with my husband when I got married. But Rule made me cum with just his finger and tongue. And when he slid inside of me.

Elle, he literally made me cum back to back. I've never experienced that before. Like… as soon as I came he just murdered my G-spot and I came again. He was so passionate and gentle yet rough and nasty. Uh. He's perfect, Elle."

"I'm so glad you finally gave him a chance. I told you he would be good for you. He's just as crazy as you but he's a sweetheart."

"He is. I took him to Edward's family dinner with me."

Elle grabbed Camryn's wrist and squeezed.

"Wait what? Family dinner? At his house?"

"Yes, child. He invited me over for Layla's fifth birthday."

"How did that turn out? Victoria didn't give you a hard time did she?"

"Nah. His wife behaved."

"I don't think I've ever heard you say that lady's name. You're petty as hell, Cam."

Camryn rolled her eyes and sat back in her seat as she crossed her ankles.

"Whatever. She was trying to be nice so I was cool. I was waiting for her ass to let some slick shit rip but she didn't."

"Well that's good. What did Aunty say about it?"

"She wanted me to go. She's going to talk to Edward this week. He's got some shit he needs to get off his chest."

"Better late than never I guess." Camryn shrugged as her thoughts went to her mother. "Are you going out with me tonight? Rule wants to take Power out for drinks and I don't want to be bored while he's gone."

"Shit if they're going out for drinks we're going out too!"

"God, I missed you, boo."

"I missed you too. I've been waiting forever to tell you about me and Rule."

"I'm so happy for you. You finally have that perfect mix of gentleman and hood nigga. I trust him with you. That's saying a lot."

Camryn blushed as Rule filled her thoughts. Never in a million years would she have thought that she would not only be in a relationship but that she would be growing in love with a man like Rule, but each day that she was with him he was showing her that change was good. And most of the things she'd been avoiding out of fear held more weight in her life than she ever imagined.

No Big Deal

Instead of going home to prepare for her night with Elle, Camryn packed a bag and went over to Rule's home. She prepared dinner for them – grilled chicken breasts, grilled tomatoes and corn, and fresh steamed green beans. Rule hadn't allowed her to go inside of his bedroom the entire time she was there because he had a surprise for her... but she had a surprise for him as well.

As Camryn put the last few utensils in the dishwasher, Rule wrapped his arms around her waist and kissed the back of her neck. She bit down on her bottom lip and placed her hands on the edge of the sink as his tongue rolled around her neck.

Rule pulled her hair, arching her neck, and bit down on it.

Camryn lifted her arm and gripped his neck from behind. Pulling him deeper into her.

"You ready for your surprise?" Rule asked into her ear before sticking his tongue inside and biting down on it.

She squirmed and pushed him away as tiny bumps covered her skin.

"I'm ready for this dick," Camryn mumbled while untying his sweatpants.

Rule looked down at Camryn with fascination as she pushed his pants and boxers down.

This woman… was simple yet complex. Hard but soft. Open yet closed and full of secrets. With each passing day he learned more about her… but there was still so much he knew he had to find out. There was something in her eyes… her demeanor… her speech and tone at certain points during conversations that told him that there was more to her than what she presented herself to be.

She was not just a biracial woman with a fascination for African American culture and history.

She was not just a teacher who wanted to be a positive influence in the lives of young girls.

She was not just a bruised heart who had trouble trusting and loving.

There was something… something under the surface of her… that pulled at the valves of his heart like magnets.

Rule grabbed her by her neck and pulled her into his body. He slid his hand up and caressed her lips with his thumb.

"These eyes, Camryn… you lock a nigga down with these eyes. I need a daughter with these eyes."

Camryn smiled and opened her mouth to respond but he closed it with his lips. At this point… he couldn't stomach her turning him down.

Rule slid his tongue into her mouth and she wrapped her arms around him immediately. He lifted her from the floor and wrapped her legs around him. After sitting her on the edge of the table, Rule pulled her shorts and panties down as she relieved herself of her shirt.

"Rule…"

"No," he interrupted.

This was not a conversation that he wanted to have right now. He wanted to enjoy the inside of her not argue about their future.

"But I…"

His entrance inside of her stole her words and replaced them with quivering lips and a quiet moan. Rule used one hand to position her flat on her back and the other to pull her ass off the table.

"Rule… will you listen to me?" She asked as he lifted her legs and placed her ankles on the tops of his shoulders.

"No," he replied honestly before diving deep inside of her.

"Fuuuuuck," she whimpered as he reached a deepness she never knew existed. A pit no man had explored before.

"Shit," he whispered, grabbing her hands and lifting her arms over her head.

With steady strokes Rule moved in and out of Camryn with a gentle and slow urgency. As if he couldn't wait to get to his destination… but my God he was enjoying the journey.

Camryn watched as Rule opened and closed his eyes. Gripped and released her legs. Bit on her ankles and muttered words and praises so low she couldn't understand him.

The pleasure consuming him overtook her. Her back arched. Her walls clenched him tighter. They heated. Tingled. Pulsed. Her legs began to tremble and fall without her permission.

"Keep them legs up. Don't mess up my strokes," he ordered holding her legs tighter.

Camryn grabbed the back of her thighs and pulled them open wider and closer to her body.

Rule leaned down and kissed her deeply. Circling his tongue around hers until she bit down on it in pleasure. He moaned into her lips as she clawed and squeezed his back.

She began to squeeze his manhood again and he lifted himself from her. Trying to distance himself from her and her orgasm to avoid his.

Camryn moaned and wrapped her legs around his waist to keep from letting them fall.

"Yes, Rule, yes. Ohmygoodness…" she slurred as she surrendered to her orgasm.

"Ummm," he moaned speeding up his strokes – coming right along with her.

Rule laid down on her and regulated his breathing while she stroked his back softly. When his heartbeats slowed down he lifted himself and stared down at the mess they'd made.

Her cream covered his manhood and thighs.

"Rule," Camryn almost whispered regaining his attention.

"Yes, baby?"

"You really want me to have your baby?"

Rule grabbed her hand and helped her get off the table.

"Do you?" She asked louder.

They walked to his room quietly as he thought about his reply.

"I do… but I know we're taking things slow while you figure this shit out."

"I'd love to."

He stopped walking and looked at her.

"You would?"

She nodded and smiled. "Yes. After we're married of course. And you leave the streets. I'm not raising no kids without my man."

"Really?"

"Really."

"Why?"

Camryn shrugged and took a step forward to restart their walk to his room.

"I want to experience you… us… on every level. I want to be your friend. Your girlfriend. Your wife. The mother of your child. Your life and purpose partner. I want to be all of that for you."

"Damn. I wasn't expecting that. I don't even know what to say."

"What did you think I was going to say?"

Rule placed his hand on the bedroom doorknob, but didn't open it.

"I thought your ass was gone just straight up say no."

She chuckled and shook her head. "Rule, I told you I was committed to this. To us. It might take us some time… but I want all of that with you. And only you. I don't want this shit with nobody else."

Rule blushed and kissed her forehead before opening the door. He stood on the side and let her walk in first to gauge her reaction to his surprise.

Her hands covered her mouth as she walked over to his bed. Carefully she ran her fingers along the yellow vinyl player.

"Is this mine?" She asked turning her attention to the crate of vinyl records next to it.

"Yeap."

"Rule... why are you so thoughtful? You take my thoughts and turn them into reality. Something I can touch. And feel. And experience."

"I just... like to see you smile. No big deal."

"That is a big deal, Rule. That's a very big deal."

He smiled and took a step back. "You gone meet me in the shower?"

"Yes, but I want to tell you about my surprise first."

"Tell me in the shower," he whined grabbing her hand and leading her to the bathroom.

"No, baby. That's gone distract me."

"Fine." Rule stopped walking and faced her. "What?"

"So... you remember how you were saying you wanted to start a nonprofit for the young niggas?"

"...Yea?"

"Well…" Camryn left the room and returned with a piece of paper. "I signed you up for a class on starting a nonprofit. It's a thirty-hour course. They'll teach you all the basics. How to apply for grants and shit. Fundraising. Creating your bylaws. Everything you need to know and do. By the time the course is over you will have completed all of the necessary steps and docs to start your nonprofit."

Rule took the paper from her hand and looked it over briefly before staring into her eyes.

She smiled and lowered her head.

He lifted it by her chin.

"You keep a nigga focused, Camryn. You don't know how much I need that shit. Thank you so much, baby. When do I start?"

"In two weeks."

His lips covered hers and he slid his hands into her hair. After kissing her until his manhood grew, Rule pulled himself away from her lips and led her to the bathroom – ready to show her just how much he appreciated what she'd done for him.

You Bring out the Man and God in Me

"So how are you going to handle it?" Power asked.

He and Rule were having drinks at L.O.V.E and Rule was filling him in on Marcel's scheme. When Rule held his meeting he was given two names to look into but neither of them came back with anything. The only person he knew for sure that was coming for him was Marcel and he was nowhere to be found.

Word was spreading that Marcel was setting up shop in North Memphis but Rule hadn't been able to get in touch with him or set eyes on him since he'd been back in Memphis.

"I'm gone end him as soon as I see him, but I need to know who he has working for him. It won't do me any good to get rid of him and then turn around and have to deal with this shit all over again. Yancey said he saw four bodies on the roof when they were shooting at him."

"Have you talked to the old heads about it yet?"

"Yea. I talked to Brandon and Tony. They gave me a couple of leads but they fell through. I've been thinking of a way to set the niggas up, but now that they know that I know what Marcel was up to everybody been on hush."

"What Pops say?"

"He don't want me to retaliate. He wants me to let the shit go."

"Why won't you?"

Rule looked at Power as if he couldn't believe Power had asked him that. He shook his head and downed the rest of his Fireball before answering.

"What I'm gone look like letting a nigga get away with that? He stole my product, tried to steal one of my clients, *and* shot at Yancey."

Power sighed and ran his hand over the waves in his hair. "So I need to join you until this shit is taken care of then?"

"Nah, big bro. I got this. You're legit now. You're married now. I got this."

"I would never be able to forgive myself if something happened to you and I wasn't there to protect you, Rule."

"Ain't nothing gone happen to me."

"I know because I'm riding with you."

"No, Power. I got it."

Power shook his head adamantly before pulling his phone out.

"Nah. I trust you and shit and I know you can handle it… but I'll be able to sleep better knowing we were in this together. That's how it's been in the past and that's how it's gone always be."

"Power…"

"End of discussion, young nigga. You know how we do. The quicker we settle this shit the quicker I can get out of it. Set up a meeting with your niggas and I'll bring Sam."

"Sam? I thought he retired? He's still being paid to watch people's body language to see if they're lying?"

"Nah, but he owes me a favor."

"Cool. I'll set it up for tomorrow morning."

"Cool. Uh… you got company."

Rule looked from Power to the direction he was looking. He closed his eyes and inhaled deeply at the sight of Diana. Praying silently that she would speak and keep it moving. He gave her a quick once over before motioning for the bartender to refill his drink.

"Hey, Rule," Diana spoke as she squeezed between his legs.

"Watch out," Rule ordered as he closed his legs, pushing her back in the process.

Diana moved to the side of him and leaned against the bar.

With attitude thick in her voice she asked, "You can't speak?"

"What's up?" Rule replied nonchalantly.

"You still throwing me shade? Or are we back friends since you're home now?"

Rule chuckled and looked at Power who was deep in his phone avoiding eye contact.

"I told you I had a lady, Diana. Gone on with that bullshit."

"You were serious about that?"

"Dead."

"So that's it?"

Instead of answering her Rule looked at her briefly and took a sip of his drink. When she didn't take the hint and leave he sighed and ran his hands down his face.

"That's it, Diana."

"Why, though? I was nothing but good to you."

"I ain't saying you weren't but I don't want you. I'm good where I'm at. You're a beautiful woman so I'm sure you won't have any trouble snatching somebody else."

"Who's your friend?" Her eyes landed on Power.

"Married," Power mumbled quickly.

"Fine. I'll let you go. Can I get a hug goodbye?" Diana opened her arms and Rule crossed his. "Come on, Rule. Don't be like that. Give me my closure so I can let you go. Get up and give me a hug goodbye."

Rule stood hesitantly and Diana took a step back to give him room. She pulled him into her by his shirt and wrapped her arms around his neck. Instead of putting her body close to his she stared into his eyes.

"Don't lose my number, Rule. I'm here whenever you want me." He nodded and tried to remove his arms but she kept them there. "Hug me like you mean it."

"Mane..."

"Please, Rule."

Rule mumbled under his breath as he pulled her closer.

"Let this be the last time you talk to me when you see me," he said into her ear. "I'm good with who I'm with. I mean that shit, Diana."

Diana snickered and grabbed his face before kissing him hard and quick.

"Oh shit," Power said.

Rule pushed Diana away and looked at Power. He closed his eyes immediately at the sight of Camryn out the corner of his eye.

"Go, Diana," Rule warned.

"For what?"

Before he could answer Camryn had a handful of Diana's hair and was about to punch her but she stopped herself and swung her to the side of the bar.

"So that's what we doing? We kissing bitches like you don't belong to me?" Camryn roared as she walked so close to Rule he had to take a step back.

"Camryn, she kissed me. I was telling her that I was good where I was at but she wasn't catching the fucking hint."

"Obviously your ass wasn't throwing it hard enough. The fuck are you even talking to the bitch for? Why y'all that close that she can stick her damn tongue in your mouth?"

"Her tongue wasn't in my mouth, Cam. Just calm down and let me explain the shit."

"Nah fuck that. Fuck you. Fuck that bitch. I should beat both of y'all asses. I can't believe you got me out here looking like a fool. I trusted your ass!"

Camryn turned to walk away with Rule right on her heel.

"Camryn, please. Let me explain," Rule begged as he grabbed at her hand, but she pulled herself away from him.

"I don't want to hear that shit, Rule. You promised me that you wouldn't play me. I told you I couldn't take being cheated on."

"I'm not cheating on you."

"Then what you call that?"

Rule grabbed her hand again and this time she allowed him to hold it.

"That's the chick that was blowing my phone up in Vegas. She was trying to get me back, but I told her that I was good with you. She gave me a line about giving her closure and that she would leave me alone afterwards. She asked for a hug and I gave her one. Then she kissed me."

The look that Camryn gave him made his heart ache. His heart race. He grabbed her arms and pulled her into him.

"You have to believe me. Ask Power. That was all her. I'm not cheating on you."

The tears that she'd been trying to hold in began to fall. Rule quickly wiped them away and kissed her temple.

"I'm sorry that you had to see that, but trust me when I say I don't want to have anything to do with her or anyone else."

Camryn wrapped her arms around him.

"Don't be kissing me. We gone have to wash your lips with soap."

Rule smiled and wiped her face again.

"Are we okay?"

Camryn nodded and ran her hands down his chest.

"We're good. I'm sorry. I should have just listened to you before I jumped to conclusions. When I saw her lips on you and your arms around her…"

"I'm sorry. I shouldn't have even hugged her. I just wanted to get her clingy ass out my face. But did you have to sling her across the room like that?"

She repressed her laugh as she wrapped her arms around his neck.

"She lucky I didn't punch her ass like I started to, but my beef was with you not her. You my man – not her."

Rule kissed her nose.

"Let's go home so we can wash my lips. I need to feel yours. I know you was mad and all… but that shit was sexy as hell."

"Whatever. Let another bitch kiss on you. Both of y'all gone get fucked up."

"I believe you. Trust me, I have no need for anyone else as long as I have you."

"Really?"

Rule looked behind them and threw up the peace sign to Power and Elle before grabbing her hand and heading out of the longue.

"Really. You do it for me."

"Why? How?"

"The simplest explanation… you bring out the man and the God in me. I need a woman like that. Even though your ass gave me the hardest time in life… what we have now is chill as hell. You got a nigga reevaluating life and shit. My goals.

Got me thinking about leaving the game earlier than I planned and going back to school. Not because you forcing the shit down my throat and nagging me about it, but because you accept me as I am and you're waiting for me to be better on my own. That makes a nigga *wanna* be better."

He wrapped his arm around her waist and she looked up at him with a smile. She ran the tips of her fingers under his chin before pulling his face down to hers and kissing him.

"Thank you for hearing me out and trusting me, Cam."

"It's cool. I know you ain't that crazy to be fucking around on me in public."

"I'm not gone fuck around on you period."

She nodded and lowered her eyes.

Rule was satisfied with how quickly she forgave him at the moment, but he had a feeling that this wouldn't be the last time they had a problem because of what Diana had just done.

Just Relax

Camryn's worst fear came to fruition – well… almost. It did… in her head. When she saw Rule intertwined with another woman flashes of her mother seated against the bathtub with tears streaming down her face years ago flooded her head. Camryn promised herself that she would never become so weak by love that she found herself in that position.

Although her relationship with Rule was still fresh she honestly could see herself with him for the long haul and Diana's lips on his challenged that thought. She had no intentions of forgiving him so easily or even hearing him out, but the amount of value that Rule had added to her life outweighed his brief moment of infidelity.

Had he cheated?

Was he really done with Diana?

As outspoken and powerful as Rule was had he really allowed a woman to trick him into kissing her?

Those questions and more filled Camryn's thoughts. So much so that she could barely sleep the night before. After tossing and turning she got up before the sun and headed to the gym.

While there she called her mother's ex-husband, Anthony. If anyone could help her understand why a man cheated it would be him. He hadn't returned her call before she was leaving the gym and heading for a smoothie.

A man sat next to her. Wearing her favorite cologne. Bleu de Chanel. Rule wore it well, and there was something about the way it mixed with his natural scent that hooked her... so smelling it on someone else immediately grabbed her attention.

He turned to face her and chills literally pierced her skin. His skin was dark. Dark chocolate. His eyes were tight, dark, and expressionless. His lips were full and black, and he had a scar on the right side of his top lip.

Camryn swallowed hard and turned back frontwards. Everything about him screamed *run away*. She closed her eyes as he looked her up and down.

"You just gone look and not speak?" He asked with a voice that reminded her of Ja Rule.

She smiled timidly and turned slightly to face him.

"Hi," she spoke softly as she grabbed her phone from the counter and prepared to stand and leave.

"Don't move, Camryn."

She looked at him with widened eyes as her grip on her phone tightened.

"How do you know my name?"

"I know your man."

"Oh. Well... what's your name? I'll tell him I ran into you."

He smiled but it fell quickly.

"Marcel. I'm going to give him my message personally. You're going to help me do that."

"How?"

"You're coming with me."

Camryn chuckled and stood. Marcel pulled his gun from his waist and put it on his lap.

"Sit down, Camryn."

Camryn licked the side of her mouth and sat back down.

"Now, we're going to do this one of two ways my love. The easy way or the hard way."

"What's the easy way?"

"You willingly leave with me and come to my warehouse."

"And the hard way?"

"I force you to."

"How?"

"With this gun to your head and a bullet flying through your mother's. I got somebody sitting outside of your house right now. One phone call from me and they're at your doorstep."

"Listen, I don't know what the hell you got going on with Rule, but my mother has nothing to do with this."

"And it's up to you to make sure she stays out of it. So choose. Easy or hard?"

"Easy."

"Smart girl. Slide me your phone."

Camryn slid her phone to him on top of the counter. She watched him press a few buttons before putting it in his pocket.

"Get up," he ordered.

She stood and grabbed her purse.

"I'm going to put this gun in my waist and walk behind you. Walk to the white car parked in front of this store. If you try anything I swear to God I'm pulling this motherfucking out and putting one in the back of your skull."

Camryn nodded and watched as he stood.

"Walk."

Slowly she walked towards the door. Trying desperately to send some type of signal to those around her with her eyes, but none of them were paying her any attention.

Marcel opened the door and she walked to the car. She closed her eyes at the sight of the three men inside.

He opened the door and she got inside. When Marcel sat next to her he pulled her phone from his pocket and scrolled through her contacts.

"What is his name in your phone?" He asked.

She lowered her head as her tears dripped like rain.

"My Heart."

Shortly after she heard Rule's voice on speakerphone.

"Hey, baby," he spoke.

She opened her mouth to speak but Marcel's finger over her lips stopped her.

"Baby is busy right now. *I* want to talk to you."

A few seconds passed before Rule replied.

"Nigga, if you even cause a piece of hair on her head to frizz up…"

"Cancel your threats. I don't want to hurt her. I just wanted to make sure I had your attention and we handled this shit my way."

"The fuck you wanna do, Marcel?"

"I'll call you tonight with further instructions."

"Hell nah. You let her ass go right now!"

"I think I'm going to hold on to her for a while. Just so you know I mean business when we meet. I'll give you a call say around nine tonight."

"This is between me and you, nigga. Leave her out of this."

"Nine."

"Fine. But when you see me… you better kill me."

Marcel smiled and quickly let it fall. "We can take it there too."

"Let me… can I… talk to him?" Camryn asked lightly.

"Try some slick shit and I'm putting one in you."

"I know, damn," Camryn said as she grabbed her phone from his hand. "Baby?"

"Camryn? Are you hurt? Has he touched you?"

"No, I'm fine. I just want you to remain calm, Rule. You don't think straight when you get upset."

"How you expect me to remain calm knowing this nigga has you? I'm bout to fuck some shit up!"

"Rule, please. Just relax, baby. I'm fine. I'm gone be fine. I can handle myself. Just remain calm and level headed."

"I'm gone get you out of this, Cam. I promise you that."

She smiled as tears flooded her eyes. "I know, baby. I…"

"That's enough."

Marcel snatched the phone from her and disconnected the call. Camryn groaned and sat on her hands – resisting the urge to slap him.

"Oh you mad?"

"Shut the hell up. You got me but I don't have to talk to your ass."

This time his smile turned into a small and quiet chuckle before he returned to his natural blank face.

"I see why he likes you. You're feisty. I like that."

Camryn shook her head in disbelief as her leg shook. She crossed her arms over her chest. Rule's words were replaying in her head.

Fear is an emotion. You were created to have dominion over all things. Don't let something intangible give birth to tangible actions. Control your emotions. Don't let that shit bring you out of yourself.

With a few deep breaths she closed her eyes and released her fear. When she opened them she looked at Marcel and her top lip twitched.

She'd never been weak because of anything or anyone, and Marcel was about to learn that he'd signed up for more than what he bargained for when he took her.

The Connect

Rule stormed through Power and Elle's hallway as if he was wind and rain himself. He found them both pacing in their kitchen.

"Get me Shak. I need Marcel's address. His parents' address. Family members' addresses. I need the address for the doctor that caught this nigga out the womb," Rule ordered.

"I'm on it," Power informed. "Have you heard back from him?"

Rule shook his head no as he scratched the top of it with the butt of his gun.

"I'm about to lose my fucking cool, Power. I'm trying so hard to remain calm and at ease, but the more time passes…"

Elle grabbed Rule's hand and pulled him into the living room. Rule looked down at her impatiently as she inhaled and exhaled deeply.

"What is it?" Rule asked.

"There's something that you need to know," she whispered as if they weren't the only two people in the room.

"What, Elle?"

She ran her hands through her hair and pulled it behind her ears.

"Has Cam ever told you about her step-father?"

"Not really. Just the basics. He cheated with her mother then cheated on her. Left when she was fourteen."

"Well… that's true… but… there's more to the story. Aunty left Anthony because of his lifestyle."

"Anthony? That name sounds familiar. What lifestyle?"

"Anthony was one of the biggest drug suppliers in Memphis before he left. The only reason he left was because he's a wanted man. The only person that knows where he is… is Cam. She's been… she's his connect. She's been funding him while he's been on the run.

No one expects it to be Cam because before he left Aunty divorced him. She was tired of his cheating. Lying. He valued money, power, and respect more than loyalty and family."

"Wait… this is too much. She's funding him while he's on the run?"

"Yes. He's been on the run for six years. He reached out to her and put her in contact with his supplier in Miami. Ever since then Cam has been the middleman between Anthony and his supplier. The supplier ships the product here to Cam and Cam distributes it for Anthony. When she gets the money she takes her cut off the top and sends the rest to Anthony."

"Who is the supplier?"

"I don't know. I just wanted you to know so you would be a bit more at ease. Cam ain't the average chick. She knows how to boss up and handle herself. She needs you to remain focused and think clearly so you can help her. She's going to be okay."

"Why didn't she tell me?"

His eyebrows were wrinkled in disbelief.

"No one knows, Rule. The only reason I know is because we're super close and I was with her one weekend when she had to make a drop. Her mother doesn't even know. The only reason she's helping him is because she feels obligated to.

We can't have you running around here like a loose cannon. I want her back just as bad as you do... but you need to calm down and remain rational and logical. You can't go on a fucking killing spree while he has her. You do that when we get her back."

"I hear you. I... I know she's a strong woman, Elle... but she's a woman. *My* woman. I can't rest until she's away from him. This is my fault. I have to fix this shit."

"No, it's not your fault. This is all Marcel. Why does this nigga have it in for you anyway?"

Rule sat his gun on the coffee table then sat down.

"I don't even fucking know. I guess he wants my throne. You know it takes nothing for a nigga to hate on the next man."

"Well... you know Power's got your back. I'm not allowed to go, but he's riding with you. I'll be praying. Just... be easy, Rule. Don't be reckless and jeopardize her life."

"I will. I won't. Marcel said he was going to call and let me know his location at nine. What time is it?"

Elle pulled her phone from her pocket and checked the time.

"Five minutes after nine."

Rule groaned and began to pace.

"Power, have you gotten in touch with Shak yet?" He yelled into the kitchen.

"He's working on getting the addresses now," Power assured him.

Rule grabbed a blunt from the fireplace and stepped outside. After lighting up he sat down and replayed his conversation with Elle over in his head.

Camryn was a connect?

That would explain why she accepted him and hadn't tried to change him. She was in the business herself.

Had Marcel been using Rule to get to Camryn all along?

Rule shook his head adamantly and stood.

"Nah, that can't be it," he whispered to himself.

He went back into the house and found Elle.

"What is Anthony's last name?"

"Barnes."

Rule did a google search on Barnes and pulled up his profile on America's Most Wanted.

"I need to talk to him."

"Why? You don't think he had something to do with this do you?"

"No, but I want to make sure Marcel isn't doing this to get to him. It's funny that he waited until I was in Vegas with her to try me. If she's a connect she probably has sold to him before without even knowing it."

"I don't know how to get in touch with him. Only Cam knows."

Rule's phone vibrated against his leg and he pulled it from his pocket promptly. Camryn's face on his phone made his heart stop beating momentarily. He inhaled a long breath and tried to compose himself as he answered.

"You're late."

"My apologies. Camryn is so damn stubborn. She just refuses to tell me what I want to hear."

"What could you possibly need to hear from her?"

"Yes. Just a simple yes."

"Yes for what, nigga? Where are you?"

"I guess you can meet me now. Try some funny shit and Camryn is dead. So is her mother."

"I won't. Just tell me where you are and what you want."

"I want your life for hers."

Rule pulled the phone away from his ear and massaged his temple. What would have probably been something not up for negotiation... or something that would have required some thought... pulled an immediate answer from Rule.

"Fine. What's the address?"

"Head to the warehouse complexes on Shelby Dr. and Hickory Hill. I'll give you the exact address when you get outside."

Rule disconnected the call and went to the kitchen with Power.

"He called. He wants me for her."

Power dug in his ear – as if there was something inside blocking him from hearing correctly.

"What you say?"

"He wants me for her."

Power stood. "There has to be a way for everyone involved to walk out. We'll think on the way, but we for damn sure ain't exchanging life for life."

"I don't want you to go, Power. I'm sending a group text to Yancey and the boys to meet me there, but I want you to stay away."

Power chuckled and shook his head casually before walking past Rule to Elle. He covered her cheek with his hand and kissed her lovingly.

"I love you, Legs. I'll see you in a few."

"I love you too. Bring my boo back."

Power nodded and looked back at Rule.

"Let's go get your woman, nigga."

Whatever I gotta do

Camryn's arms and legs were crossed. Her willingness to cooperate was just as closed up and defensive as her body was. The entire time she'd been at the warehouse Marcel had been trying to force her to know information she had no idea about.

It was true – Camryn *was* working for her step-father. When he left their home when she was fourteen she thought she would never see him again or hear from him again, but he continued to provide for them financially.

When it was time for Camryn to enroll in college, Anthony wrote her a check that was big enough to cover her tuition for four years and cover room and board. His generosity surprised her, and made her curious.

As far as she knew, Anthony had his own heating and air business.

Before she started school Camryn reached out to Anthony. It was then that she found out how he really made his money. That her mother left him because she refused to be his main chick while he slept around with any and everyone else he came in contact with on the streets.

While he put his life and freedom and that of hers and Camryn's on the line. While he not only sold but experimented with the drugs he supplied.

Him paying for her schooling made her appreciate him, but their personal relationship still was nonexistent because of how he treated her mother.

A couple of weeks into her first semester of college Anthony showed up at her dorm. He told her that he had to leave town to avoid going to jail and to let her mother know he would do all he could to provide for her. Without all of the details about why Anthony was about to submit himself to a life on the run Camryn asked what she could do to help.

What started off as a one-time delivery turned into a six-year gig.

Camryn thought she was careful of making sure no one knew what she was doing, but Marcel's questioning let her know that he was well aware of her involvement in the drug game.

Not only did he know that she was connected to Anthony, but he was sure that she knew the ins and outs of Rule's organization. She tried to convince him that she knew nothing about Rule's business but he didn't believe her. So her stubbornness took over and she stopped talking completely.

Now Marcel was sitting in front of her and they were engaged in what appeared to be a staring contest. He finally gave in and spoke.

"You need to tell me what I need to know before your little boyfriend gets here and gives his life for yours."

"What? No. He can't. I'm telling you I don't know shit about Rule's dealings."

"I don't believe you."

"That's not my problem."

"Oh but it is."

"Just… tell me what you want, Marcel. Is it money? We got that."

Marcel gave her that quick smile that she grew disgusted with each time she saw it.

"Maybe you don't know anything about Rule's business, but I know that you're Anthony's step-daughter. Are you his Memphis and Mid-south connect?"

Camryn sat back in her seat and ignored his question.

"I already know you are, Camryn."

"I don't know what you're talking about."

"You wanna lie? Fine. You're my key to killing two birds with one stone. I want Memphis. I want Anthony and Rule's territory."

Camryn's arms fell and she sat up in her seat.

"You're going through all of this for some damn street corners you basic ass nigga? You wanna take somebody's territory? Up your product. Get a different grade. Buy them niggas out. You don't fucking kidnap a woman and try to use her as leverage. That's some bitch ass shit!"

Marcel smiled and allowed it to linger longer than he ever had before.

"Here we go. I'm glad you're dropping your little innocent girl act. Work with me. Cut Anthony and Rule out and work solely with me."

"Never in your fucking life. And I don't work for either of them anyway."

"Fine. You wanna play this game that's cool. When Rule gets here he's giving me him for you. I'll end him tonight. Anthony will be more difficult to find, but I'll settle for having just Rule for now. Unless you want to tell me where Anthony is?"

"I don't know where he is."

Marcel stood.

"Wait… how do you think you're going to get away with killing Rule? Do you not know who he is? Who his family is?"

"My second in command has strict orders to kill them off one by one should anything happen to me after this switch is complete. I'm tired of the Owens clan running Memphis. It's time for someone new to take over. And that's gone be me."

He tried to walk away again. She stopped him again.

"Wait… is there… something we can do to work this out? I don't want him to die because of me. Please."

"Well that's going to happen regardless. But it's cute that you both care so much about each other that you're willing to go to war for each other."

"Think smart, Marcel. If you kill Rule you will have niggas coming at you from all sides. Is that a battle that you really want to start? Let me help you get out of this with your life."

Marcel smiled and sat back down.

"I tell you what. You're Anthony's connect… right?"

Camryn placed her elbows on her knees and put her face inside of her palms.

"Are you?"

"Yes." Camryn lifted her face and met his eyes. "Yes."

"Good girl. I do have a plan B. Should I need to execute it I'll need forty keys from you, one hundred thousand dollars, and a clear path out of Memphis."

"Are you fucking serious? Forty keys? That's eighty thousand in the streets! You think I got that type of weight just sitting around in my house?"

"Don't bullshit me, Camryn. Anthony is a big time supplier. He only supplies to middle and big time dealers. I know he's moving at least ten to twenty keys a month. Probably double that. If you want to secure Rule's life those are my terms."

Camryn chuckled in disbelief and quickly ran a count of the product she had in storage through her head. What she didn't have Rule would have to add to. *Rule*. How was she going to explain this to him?

"So let me get this straight… Rule dies and you take over Memphis, or I give you forty keys and a hundred stacks and you leave Memphis and set up shop somewhere else?"

Marcel nodded.

"How can I trust that you won't come back to Memphis and try to keep me on a leash?"

"I'm a man of my word."

"And that's supposed to mean something to me?"

"If you want Rule to walk out of here it should."

All of her late night conversations with Rule were drowning her brain. This wasn't how they were supposed to end. Rule was supposed to leave the game. She was going to leave the game. Rule was going to return to college. She was going to finish her PhD journey. They were going to get married and have babies with a farm full of fresh food and lots of animals.

"Whatever I gotta do to walk out of here with him I will," Camryn agreed.

"Now… was that so hard?"

"Fuck you."

Rule

Rule, Power, Yancey, and seven other men walked into Marcel's warehouse strategically. Rule sent two the left and two to the right. Two stayed at the doors while the rest walked inside. The second Rule laid eyes on Camryn he reached for his gun but Power stopped him.

"Don't shoot. Stick to the plan," Power muttered.

Rule nodded and walked towards her. Marcel stepped in front of her and pointed his gun at Rule. Power, Yancey, and Brandon drew their guns.

"I'm here. Now let her go," Rule ordered.

"I need you to step back like ten feet." Marcel smiled and motioned for Rule to step back.

"Do it, Rule. Please," Camryn begged.

Rule stepped back until he was next to Power.

Marcel turned to Camryn and told her to stand up.

"Do we have a deal?" Camryn asked with her back to Rule.

Marcel looked her over and took a step back.

"I... I don't think so. Go kiss your man goodbye."

"Marcel, think. Are you sure you want to start this war? You will not win."

"I need you on my team, Camryn."

Rule pulled his gun and aimed it at Marcel as multiple guns cocked simultaneously. He looked up and around the warehouse and counted five men that he didn't know plus his own crew.

"Rule, please. Lower your gun," Camryn reasoned.

"Come here, Camryn."

Camryn looked at Marcel for permission. He nodded and turned around to face Rule. When she was standing in front of Rule he asked, "Why didn't you tell me?"

Her mouth opened and closed in surprise.

"Tell you what?"

"About Anthony."

"Can we talk about this later?"

"There may not be a later, baby. I'm sorry for getting you involved in this."

Her eyes watered. She shook her head and wrapped her arms around him as he secured his gun in his pants to hug her back.

"This isn't your fault, Rule. This goes beyond you. He… he wants your territory and Anthony's."

Rule looked over her and at Marcel.

"How you think you gone get away with that?"

Marcel smiled and released a hard breath as he looked around the warehouse.

"My second in command has strict orders to execute your family one by one if anything happens to me. Starting with your parents. Then Power and his new wife. So not only will you be dead but their murders will be on you as well."

"Who is your second in command?" Camryn asked.

"Come on now. You know I'm not telling you that."

Rule grabbed her arm and turned her around to him.

"You need to leave with Power," Rule instructed.

"Rule, I'm not leaving you here alone."

"Listen to me, Camryn. Go with Power."

"No, Rule. I'm not leaving you!"

He kissed her forehead and stared into her eyes.

"Do as I say. Trust me, okay? I love you."

"Rule… no…"

"Power, come get her."

"Rule, no. I'm not leaving you."

Rule stepped around her and in front of Marcel.

Power grabbed Camryn's arm and pulled her towards the exit.

"Power, let me go! I'm not leaving him here alone."

"Trust your man," he whispered into her ear. "Trust your man."

She looked up at Power with tear stained cheeks and nodded okay. The doors creaked open and everyone looked back as Diana entered the warehouse.

"The fuck is she doing here?" Camryn asked.

"Diana… didn't I tell you not to come until I called?" Marcel asked.

"Why do you have guns on Rule, Marcel? You told me he wouldn't be hurt. You told me she was going to cooperate and if not she was the one that would die – not Rule."

"You working for this nigga?" Rule asked stepping towards her.

"I don't work for him. He works for me. I let him have the pussy a couple of times now his head gone. He was supposed to get Anthony's territory from her and convince her to talk you out of yours and let business be business."

Diana stepped to the side and looked at Marcel.

"What are you doing, Marcel?"

"What am I doing? No… what are *you* doing? You were never supposed to have sex with him. You were never supposed to catch feelings for him. You were supposed to play him, get in and get out. But since you don't know how to handle your business I'm gone make sure he's out the way. Permanently."

"No wait… you said you were going to cut that deal with me. Forty keys and a hundred stacks in exchange for his life." Camryn said stepping up and closer to Rule.

"Wait… what? You were going to sell me out? Go behind my back and cut a different deal? That wasn't what we agreed on." Diana rushed out quickly as she pulled her gun and aimed it at Marcel. "I knew I shouldn't have trusted your filthy ass."

Marcel extended his gun.

Rule pulled his.

Power shot his.

Camryn leaped towards Rule.

Marcel's bullet connected with Camryn's back before Power's connected to his skull.

Rule grabbed Camryn and pulled her behind a large bin as gunfire blasted from all over. Diana tried to make a run for it, but Power's two shots to her knees stopped her. He pulled her behind the bin and tried his best to avoid Rule's distressed face.

"Rule, call 911 and get her an ambulance. I need to get Diana out of here to make sure she doesn't lose too much blood. We need her. If they have eyes on our folks along with Camryn's mom she's more beneficial alive than dead."

"She... did she just... she took a fucking bullet for me?" Rule asked in disbelief as he rocked with Camryn's bloody body in his lap.

"Rule... listen to me, baby. I need you to call 911," Power spoke in a softer tone.

"Camryn... Camryn... why would you do that? Why would you do that? I need you to stay awake for me," Rule pleaded as he pulled his phone from his pocket.

"I'm carrying Diana out the back. Yancey and Brandon will cover y'all until I get back. Call them and get them over here, Rule. She's going to be fine," Power assured him before picking Diana up and carrying her outside.

"Camryn... can you hear me, baby?" Rule asked as tears filled and fell from his eyes.

Her eyes fluttered softly as she fought to keep them open. Camryn grabbed the sleeve of his shirt weakly before releasing it.

"I... love you... too..." she whispered.

"Camryn, keep your eyes open for me, baby."

Rule dialed 911 finally and placed kisses all along her face.

"Yea... I'm at 5695 Shelby Dr. I'm in the big white warehouse with green trim. I need like... shit I don't know how many ambulances... but y'all need to get here quick!"

The phone dropped from his shaking hand as he watched Camryn's eyes close and not reopen.

"Camryn..." He called as he shook her gently. "Baby..."

Still no response. He checked her pulse. The faint beat of her heart made his eyes literally see red. Rule kissed her once more before laying her body on the floor and going back into the gunfire to dance with Satan since it seemed as if all hell had just broken loose.

Power crept back in just in time enough to see Rule walking directly into the barrage of bullets.

"Rule... Rule!!"

To be continued...